"I really ... we find Valerie."

Shelby continued a little shyly. "It's more than just talking to her about another book. It sounds silly, I know, but after writing to her for almost three years, losing her is a blow." She stared at the braided rug, feeling as if she'd bared her soul to this man who would probably think her foolish.

She didn't look up. She was afraid of what she might see in those devilishly dark eyes.

"I hope you find her, too," Mark said tenderly as he slipped an arm around her shoulder and kissed her. "You looked as if you were about to cry," he said when he let her go. "I thought if you slapped me it would make you forget your troubles."

"But I didn't want to slap you...."

Mark smiled slowly. "I know."

Leigh Michaels is married to "the best photographer in the United States," and in 1979 they published a photo book, *Pilgrimage*, documenting the Pope's visit to Des Moines, Iowa. She believes all good writing is actually rewriting and confesses to having sent a quarter of a million words up in smoke herself, but who's counting? Leigh holds a degree in journalism and teaches now and then at a community college. Her family includes two teenagers, a cross-bred mutt who thinks he's human and a Siamese "aristo-cat." Leigh loves to write and has enough ideas for romance to keep her busy for a long time.

Books by Leigh Michaels

HARLEQUIN ROMANCE
2657—ON SEPTEMBER HILL
2734—WEDNESDAY'S CHILD
2748—COME NEXT SUMMER

HARLEQUIN PRESENTS
702—KISS YESTERDAY GOODBYE
811—DEADLINE FOR LOVE
835—DREAMS TO KEEP
876—TOUCH NOT MY HEART
900—LEAVING HOME

Capture a Shadow

Leigh Michaels

Harlequin Books

TORONTO • NEW YORK • LONDON
AMSTERDAM • PARIS • SYDNEY • HAMBURG
STOCKHOLM • ATHENS • TOKYO • MILAN

Original hardcover edition published in 1986
by Mills & Boon Limited

ISBN 0-373-02806-7

Harlequin Romance first edition December 1986

For Michael,
a different kind of Saint.

CHAPTER ONE

SHE had never before seen the Old Man so angry, and it frightened her.

As Bob Jonas paced down the office towards the chair where she huddled, Shelby Stuart tried to talk herself out of that unreasoning fear. *After all, it isn't as though he's going to strike me,* she thought. *So he's red-faced, and swearing with a fluency I would never have suspected him capable of. I'm not exactly a lightweight myself. It takes more than one irritable man to scare me.*

But as he leaned over her chair to shake a well-manicured fingernail in her face, Shelby shrank back into the deep upholstery. She cursed the primitive instinct of self-preservation that had made her flinch, and tried to regain her position.

'In my judgment, Mr Jonas——' she began.

He whirled around from the desk. 'You have no judgment!' he snapped. 'Your position here is an accident, Miss Stuart!'

'Mr Jonas——'

He banged a fist down on the newspaper that lay open on his desk. 'Did you or did you not send Natasha Winslow's last manuscript back to her?'

'I did, but——'

'And did she or did she not submit it to another publisher, who jumped at the chance to print it?'

'Yes, but——'

'And is it or is it not at the top of the *New York Times* paperback best-seller list this week?'

'I haven't any idea,' Shelby said tartly. 'You keep waving that newspaper under my nose, but you haven't yet let me look at it.'

His jaw tightened. 'Take it from me, Miss Stuart—it is.' He leaned against the desk, his hands clenched on the edge. 'Now, what is your justification for losing this author?'

Shelby kept her voice level with an effort. 'The book was pornographic, and she refused to tone it down.'

'Pornographic by whose standards, Miss Stuart? Yours?'

'And the industry's as well, come to that. It went far beyond the limits of taste for a romance novel, I can assure you. If you would read it yourself, Mr Jonas, I'm certain you'd agree——'

'But I can't very well do that, can I?' he said, and the sudden sweetness of his voice was more threatening than all the bluster had been. 'I can't read it, unless I walk down the street to the corner bookstore and buy it—which is the whole point! We should have published that book.'

'Believe me, Mr Jonas, it was not the kind of thing you want to be identified with this publishing firm——'

'It was written by the best-selling author in the field.'

'Oh, now I understand. You think that anything Natasha Winslow writes should be published just as it flows from an extremely cluttered mind, without benefit of editing?'

He glared at her. 'We had an exclusive arrangement with the woman until you decided abruptly that her style was too risqué——'

'The word is trashy.' Shelby's voice was clipped. 'That kind of language is suitable only for pulp fiction wrapped in brown paper and sold from under the counter.'

'And not suitable for our readers, is that what you're saying?'

'Absolutely. And I might add that when a lowly editor has to remind the head of the company of that fact——'

'That, my dear Miss Stuart, is why *you* are a lowly editor, and *I* am the head of the company.'

Shelby kept her temper with an effort, and tried to regain ground. 'At any rate, it's been a year since I sent that manuscript back. It's all long gone.'

'Not exactly,' he said, tapping his finger on the newspaper. 'It will be reminding us for years to come— every time we see Natasha Winslow's name on this list.'

Shelby shrugged. 'I did everything I could,' she pointed out. 'I'd tried for six months to tone that book down and make it something we could use. But it wasn't only the language, you understand. The lead character had hopped into bed with six different men by Chapter Five, and our readers don't want that sort of thing. They don't expect it . . .'

'Spare me the lecture,' Bob Jonas snapped. 'Frankly, I don't care what the readers like, as long as they keep buying books.'

'But don't you see? That's the whole point! They're expecting romance, and warmth, perhaps a little heavy breathing. How long will they keep buying our brand if we give them this trash instead?'

'They'll buy it because it has her name on it,' he pointed out. 'And now they're buying it from another company. That's the bottom line, Miss Stuart.'

Good riddance to Natasha Winslow, Shelby thought, and had to bite her tongue to keep from saying it.

Bob Jonas sat down behind his desk and folded his hands atop the empty blotter. 'You are on probation, Miss Stuart,' he said matter-of-factly. 'Another mistake like this one, and you're out.'

Shelby jumped up. 'You can't do this to me!' she snapped. 'I handle every million-selling author you have——'

'The ones I still have, don't you mean?' he asked pleasantly. 'Believe me, Miss Stuart, if it wasn't for people like Maria Martin and Valerie St John, you wouldn't be getting this second chance. But they're valuable authors, and I can't afford to take the chance of them leaving with you. So I'm telling you this instead: be thankful you still have your job. Mess it up one more time—lose Maria Martin or Valerie St John, or anyone else, and you're done.' He pushed the best-seller list off the desk into the wastebasket with a contemptuous finger. 'Good day, Miss Stuart.'

There was nothing more to be said. Shelby retreated to her own office, biting her tongue to keep from saying all the bitter things she'd like to express. The Old Man had not spoken a word of praise for her discovery of Maria Martin and Valerie St John. He had not given a breath of encouragement or appreciation for the hard work she did. Just a threat that would cripple her work from now on, and a dark cloud of doom that would hang over her.

She sat down at her desk, staring at nothing. 'He might as well have blindfolded me,' she muttered, 'for all the work I can do now.' What good was an editor who wasn't allowed to exercise her judgment?

'Is the Old Man in top form today?' It was another of the senior editors, coming in with a stack of mail for Shelby.

'You might say.' Shelby took one look at the two-foot-high pile of manila envelopes and shuddered. Would she dare look at a manuscript just now? What if she made another mistake?

And that's enough of that, she told herself firmly. Turning down Natasha Winslow's last novel had not been a mistake. It was the Old Man who was wrong.

'Cheer up,' the other woman said. 'You're going on vacation next week, and leaving all of us here to slave away. To say nothing of the fact that today is your lucky day.'

Shelby snorted. 'Lucky day? That's easy for you to say. You weren't the one who was just threatened——'

Then she snatched up the pale pink envelope that lay on top of the pile. 'You're right,' she said, with a sunny smile, 'it is my lucky day.'

'Wish I'd been the one who discovered Valerie,' the other editor said, and her tone was mildly envious. 'None of my people are interested in intellectual conversations, they all want to talk about money. Unless, of course, they're writing to complain about ugly cover designs, or editing changes, or contract terms.'

'I know. Valerie is the exception to everything.'

'And then they run to ten pages. If they'd spend half as much time writing chapters as they do on letters——'

'I know, I know. Valerie can say more in two paragraphs than most of them can in a book.' Shelby balanced the envelope on her fingertips. 'Are you waiting around for me to open this?'

'Of course not, I know you always insist on being alone. No one else in the whole office has to have privacy to read a letter from an author, for heaven's sake! Are you going to that cocktail party tonight at Lora Wilde's apartment?'

For an instant Shelby's entire body rebelled at the idea of standing around Lora Wilde's admittedly gorgeous apartment, balancing a champagne glass and a plate of titbits and shouting above the rumble of meaningless conversation. The cigarette smoke alone would have her head pounding in fifteen minutes. Then, reluctantly, she nodded. 'No one but a fool would miss one of Lora's parties.'

'That's what I thought. See you there.' The editor started for the door. 'Enjoy your letter.'

Besides, Shelby thought, *every publisher in New York will be represented tonight at Lora's party*. She could ask a few questions, drop a few hints—maybe find out which companies might be looking for a new editor. Lora herself might know. Lora Wilde wasn't a high-powered literary agent for nothing; she knew everyone, and every speck of gossip, in the whole business.

Shelby waited, unwilling to share the letter she held, till the editor was out of sight. Who but Valerie St John would have thought of a heart-shaped return-address label, Shelby thought as she carefully slit the envelope. It certainly got everyone's attention, and the personality that sparkled from the hot pink label compensated for the coolness of the post-office box number that was printed on it.

Shelby had commented about that, early in their correspondence. A romance writer's mail, she had protested, ought to be delivered to somewhere romantic—not to a cold post office box in a little town in the Midwest. Valerie had answered with a laugh that could be heard through the crisply typed lines of her next letter. 'After all,' she had written, 'this is the Heartland of America. What more can we ask?'

Shelby smiled, remembering. Valerie never said much about herself at all—just her work. No matter what subjects Shelby asked about, Valerie's answers were non-committal. She was a very private person, Shelby thought.

She pulled the sheet of stationery out of the envelope. She had just accepted Valerie's sixth novel; this would be the warm acknowledgment of her letter, and the progress report on number seven, which was probably well under way by now . . .

How lucky she had been, Shelby thought, on that long-ago day when she had opened a manila envelope and Valerie's first novel had slid into her hands! Her books were ones to savour and think about. They were consistently good, and so widely different that it was easy to approach the job with enthusiasm. If only some of the rest of Shelby's authors—the porno lady included—had half of Valerie's skill with words!

Shelby took a deep breath of the scented stationery.

She loved fragrances, but she wasn't sure if she liked this one so well for itself or because it had come to mean Valerie St John. It had a hint of lilacs about it, she thought, and leaned back in her chair to savour the letter.

'I'm glad you liked the novel,' Valerie had written. 'It has become my favourite, and I think it's a good note to stop on. I'm without ideas at the moment, and frankly, I'm tired. Writing these things is harder work than I ever imagined, so perhaps a year off will freshen my outlook. I'll be in touch when the sabbatical is over. In the meantime, bless you for all your help, and . . .'

The letter dropped from Shelby's nerveless hand. 'She can't do this to me,' she whispered. 'Dammit, Valerie, you can't quit now!'

But she could, of course. Her contract was fulfilled, and even if it hadn't been, there was no way to hold a whip over Valerie's head. She had merely promised to offer her work to Jonas Brothers first; no contract could force her to write faster or more than she chose.

Shelby put her throbbing head down on the desk blotter and breathed the heady scent of Valerie St John's perfume. Valerie was finished with romance novels, and because of that decision made half a continent away, Shelby Stuart was finished as an editor at Jonas Brothers. It was as simple as that.

She hoped that Lora Wilde knew of a publishing house who needed an editor right away.

The din was frightful. Shelby stood by the wide window, open to the Manhattan night, which provided nominal ventilation for the room. She took a sip from a Bloody Mary that had gone warm in her hand, and looked around at Lora Wilde's huge, luxurious apartment.

It had been redecorated again since her last visit, and this time was in restful silver and blue. Lora herself, her cloud of dark hair loose around her shoulders, was also all in silver tonight, but there was nothing restful about her. She flitted from group to group, her laugh tinkling above the rumble, a long cigarette-holder in her hand.

'Don't you ever wonder,' said a voice next to Shelby's ear, 'how Lora explains this luxury to all her clients? After all, they're paying for it with their ten per cent agent's fees.'

Shelby looked up at the tall blond man at her elbow. 'I expect she tells them the truth. After all, Lora wasn't only born with the proverbial silver spoon in her mouth—she had cutlery for twelve.'

'Ah? Not fair, is it, Shelby? All this and she's pretty, too.'

Shelby shrugged. 'I never thought about it, Rodney. Lora is a friend—I don't waste my time being jealous of my friends.'

He shook his head. 'You won't make it far in the cut-throat world of publishing if you take friendship at face value, Shelby.'

He should know, she thought drily. Rodney didn't have a friendship in the world that wasn't milked for all the connections he could possibly make.

'Oh, look,' he said. 'There's Natasha.'

Shelby looked around with distaste. Natasha Winslow had paused in the doorway, her scarlet sequinned gown fitted so tightly to her voluptuous curves that Shelby wondered vaguely how the woman had managed to sit down in a taxi. Over her shoulder was a fur boa, despite the warmth of September's Indian summer. Her makeup was theatrical and heavy, and from across the room Shelby could see the stark eyeliner and the long false eyelashes. The woman was nearing forty, but her makeup artist was using every trick in the book to hold off the dreaded day as long as possible.

'On her new promotional tour, I suppose,' Shelby said coolly.

'That's right. We're really promoting her new novel. I'm sure you saw it on the best-seller list this week.'

Shelby's jaw tightened. Rodney never missed an opportunity to remind her that his company was Natasha's new publisher. 'She certainly draws attention, dressed that way.'

'Meee-ow,' Rodney murmured. 'Just because the lady is no longer writing for you is no reason to be catty, Shelby. Try dressing for success yourself some time. You might be surprised what would happen if you stopped hiding in corners.'

He was right, Shelby thought reluctantly. Natasha Winslow was shrewd enough to know that only extremes drew the kind of attention she wanted—the kind that sold books. And he was equally right about herself. She had always felt stifled at cocktail parties, and she preferred tailored jackets to sequins. Her figure was adequate, her ash-blonde hair had a natural glow, and her eyes—her one unique feature—were precisely Williamsburg blue. But in a roomful of gorgeous women, Shelby thought, who was going to pay attention to one more blue-eyed blonde?

Maybe Rodney was right, she thought. Perhaps she was just a tiny bit jealous of the Lora Wildes and the Natasha Winslows of the world. It was a sobering thought.

'Have you heard who her latest conquest is?' Rodney asked, drawing her towards the bar and handing his empty glass to the bartender.

'Natasha's?' Shelby shook her head as he raised an eyebrow towards her glass. 'No more, thanks. Who cares who Natasha sleeps with? We'll all know next year when the new book comes out, that's sure. He'll have a starring role.'

'You wouldn't be a woman if you didn't want to know,' Rodney pointed out. He sipped his drink appreciatively. 'Besides which, if you're nice to me you won't have to wait till the book comes out. I've already read it. Tell you what, I'll trade you all the inside dirt about Natasha for one tiny bit of information——'

'Let me guess, you want Valerie St John's address.' It wasn't the first time he had tried to pry that knowledge from her. The publishing firm Rodney worked for would give a great deal more than gossip if they could buy Valerie away from Jonas Brothers. Shelby had reached the point where she found it humorous in a tired sort of way.

'Phone number, actually,' Rodney said with a sleek smile.

She raised an eyebrow. 'Sorry, Rodney, trade secret. Surely you aren't surprised?'

'That you won't give it to me? No. Rumour has it that the lovely Valerie has not divulged all her vital statistics even to you.'

Shelby wondered how that bit of information had leaked. How had Rodney known that her request for a telephone number where Valerie could be reached had been politely turned down?

It made her a little angry, but it wasn't unusual for such knowledge to have spread, she knew. The publishing industry was a hotbed of speculation, and Jonas Brothers was no exception.

It would serve the Old Man right, she thought, if she did tell Rodney in which little town he could find Valerie St John. But it wouldn't be kind to the writer herself. Rodney was all right, even if he was a bit of a stuffed shirt, but the line of books his company put out were hardly of the consistent quality that Jonas Brothers produced, and Valerie would not be happy there, so Shelby dismissed the thought with regret. One did, after all, owe something to one's friends, she thought. Even if Valerie's action might cost her her job . . .

'Are you out to lunch?' Rodney asked briskly. 'Or are

you running through a list of staff members, trying to figure out who ratted?'

'When you've been around a little longer,' she said in a purposely patronizing tone, 'you'll learn not to believe everything you hear.'

He laughed. 'How about having dinner with me over the weekend and we'll discuss it?'

'Sorry, I'm off on vacation come Saturday.'

'Something exciting?'

She hesitated, then told the truth. 'A New England tour. I've never seen it at this season, so——'

'Ugh! Watch the leaves turn red, that sort of thing?' Rodney shivered. 'Give me another drink.' He grinned and moved away towards the bar.

He was satisfied, Shelby thought. He'd got in his usual digs and unsettled her evening, that was all he had wanted. She was glad for the easy excuse to avoid having dinner with him. According to Bob Jonas, cultivating the enemy was part of Shelby's job— picking up whatever titbits might fall if Rodney was less than careful with his drinks—but of course, the reverse of that was also true; Shelby had to watch her tongue carefully. The result was a war of nerves that always left her quivering by evening's end.

She set her glass aside and made her way to the powder room, where it might be a little quieter, if no less smoky. At least there she would only have to cope with the female of the species.

She kicked off her shoes and sank into a white wicker chair. Lora must be the only woman in New York who had a powder room built for a crowd, Shelby thought idly, and with this redecoration it had turned into a tropical jungle. She pulled a compact out of her handbag and winced as a crackle of paper and a drift of lilac perfume touched her senses.

Valerie St John's letter lay at the bottom of her handbag like a ticking time bomb. She hadn't dared to leave it at the office; someone was always dashing in to check her files. She couldn't even lock it in her desk because that would have created the very suspicion she wanted to avoid.

She propped her elbows on the arms of the chair and massaged her temples, trying to work out what to do. The entire office knew there had been a letter today. That in itself was no problem, because Valerie's letters were seldom passed around. If asked, Shelby could say that the letter had just expressed happiness that the book had been satisfactory. No one would expect another manuscript for months; in fact, sometimes it was that long between Valerie's letters. It was one of the charmingly unexpected things about the woman; there would be letters every week for a while, and then it would seem that she had dropped off the face of the earth for a month or two at a time.

I'll send her a letter, Shelby thought. *I'll tell her how very important it is that she write just one more book for me. Even if she'll only pretend to write another one—if she'll just keep writing letters, so that everything looks normal for a while——*

She was beginning to sound panic-stricken, she reminded herself. If she could just keep her head for one month and pretend that all was well, she was sure Valerie would get her off the hook.

If, she thought, this wasn't one of those times that Valerie disappeared. In any case, Shelby thought, I'm only buying time. The Old Man has made up his mind that I've got to go——

That's defeatist thinking, she told herself roundly. She had to try at least. So she swallowed hard and started composing her letter to Valerie St John in her mind.

She was just finishing a passionate appeal that would have melted the heart of the Abominable Snowman himself when Lora came into the powder room in a swirl of silver tissue. 'I thought you'd disappeared,' she said. 'You aren't ill, are you?'

'No, I'm fine.'

'Well, do come out of the john or I'll have to start charging you rent. Everyone's gone home.'

Shelby glanced at her watch. 'Oh—I am sorry. I sort of lost track of the time. I was—ummm—admiring your plants.'

Lora lifted one elegantly-shaped eyebrow. 'My decorator will be flattered beyond words,' she said. 'Let's have coffee, and raid the refrigerator. Unless you have somewhere else to go?'

Shelby's stomach reminded her that she had passed by the table of hors-dœuvres, Lora's sudden down-to-earth sanity relaxed her tension, and she smiled. 'Come to think of it, I hadn't planned a thing.'

'The caterers left everything, of course. I'm sure we can find enough to nibble on.'

The rooms looked absurdly big, with the clutter of a hundred guests scattered from end to end. 'Leave it,' Lora said with a wave of her hand, 'let's retreat to the kitchen where it's clean.'

They found a deli platter in the refrigerator. 'Devastating to my diet, you know,' Lora said with a smile, as she assembled a motley sandwich and drizzled horseradish sauce over it.

'Also devastating to your diamond rings. Do be careful, Lora, or you'll get crumbs down in those tiny cracks and your jeweller will never speak to you again.'

'I know,' Lora sighed. 'He got very angry with me when I cut my fingernails. Said my rings deserved a better display than this! But really, Shelby, I couldn't type when they were two inches long, and one does have to make a living.'

'Haven't you found a secretary yet?'

'None that suits me.'

'Where do I file an application?'

There was a brief silence while Lora finished off her sandwich and helped herself to potato salad. 'I thought there must be a reason for you to be hiding in the powder room.'

Shelby told her. 'I'm in deep trouble,' she finished. 'Unless you know of someone who needs a good editor——'

Lora sighed. 'And I thought it was just another unsuitable man and freshly broken heart.'

'Lora, I haven't fallen for a man in at least six weeks.'

'How well I remember, darling. I thought even you would draw the line at the stand-up comic—I know, he was cute. If you'd just find a suitable man——'

'One with money?' Shelby interrupted.

'Of course.' Lora was unperturbed. 'Then you could tell Bob Jonas to go jump into the East River. But instead, you keep dating all these freaks.' She looked at Shelby thoughtfully and added, 'I know some really nice young men, Shelby. If you'd just let me set you up——'

'You know that every time you arrange a blind date for me, it falls flat,' Shelby reminded. 'They all expect me to be like you.'

'Not all of them,' Lora demurred. 'There was the stockbroker——'

Shelby rolled her eyes. 'Oh yes, I remember the stockbroker. Well, I've never met a stockbroker—or anyone else, for that matter—who would put up with the hours I work.'

'Slave labour,' Lora murmured.

'I do it because I like it! And if you're going to suggest that I quit working altogether—no, thanks. Even if I could afford not to work, I like my job far better than most men I've met. At least I would, if Bob Jonas would leave me alone and let me work.'

'There is that problem,' Lora mused.

'At any rate, Lora, I need a new job, not a man.'

'That's what you think, dear.' She thought it over and shrugged. 'It's tight right now,' she warned. 'No one is hiring. I know a dozen good people who are out of jobs at the moment.'

'Please, Lora, must you be so encouraging about it?'

'And nobody wants an editor with a reputation for making trouble, which you'd have if you left Jonas Brothers just now. You'd better stay right where you are for the present. We can keep our ears open, and as soon as the right job appears——'

'But don't you see? I don't have the luxury of time, unless Valerie St John will produce one more book for me. I'm going to write to her tonight, but——'

'Why waste time on a letter? Don't be proud—call the woman and beg. Do it right now.'

'That's just it. She never gave me her phone number.'

'Haven't you heard of directory information? Really, Shelby.' Lora reached for the telephone that was never more than an arm's length away from her. 'Which town?' she asked, the handle of her spoon poised over the dial so she wouldn't scratch the lacquer on her nails.

Shelby sighed and told her. There was no use arguing with Lora.

Ten minutes later she put the phone down and bit her elegantly painted lip. 'There is no one named St John in that town, Shelby.'

'If you would have listened to me, I could have told you that. It's her pen name—everybody uses them, and so long as our writers produce for us, we don't care what they call themselves.'

'You don't even know the woman's name?' Each word was crisply enunciated and unbelieving.

'We never needed to know. If Valerie St John didn't want to tell us——' Shelby shrugged. 'It was really none of our business.'

'The only thing you have is a post-office box number?'

'That's right.'

Lora scowled, threatening her perfect skin. 'Don't panic, darling,' she drawled, 'but I think you're in the soup. If she isn't planning to write any more, what makes you think she'll even keep the post-office box?'

'That's how we pay her royalties.'

Lora lit a cigarette. The long holder gleamed silver in her hand. 'And when is the next cheque due?' she said, blowing a cloud of smoke.

'Three months. It's——' Shelby stopped dead. 'You don't think she'll even look at the mail in the meantime, do you?'

'Would you?' Lora asked drily. 'The next letter she gets from you will be a plea, which is exactly what she doesn't want to hear. Besides, she may have gone off on a world cruise or something.'

'Valerie's not the type.'

'Just what do you know about this woman?'

'Well——' Shelby thought about it. 'She's very clever with words, she likes to play with them. She doesn't like French food——'

'That should come in handy, since she insists on living in the back of beyond,' Lora mused. 'Which reminds me, there's something familiar about that town . . .' She thought about it, her eyes half-closed, her head tilted back, smoke hovering around her head. 'Warren's Grove . . . I've heard of it before.'

'Not from me. You're the first person I've ever told that much about Valerie St John,' Shelby warned, 'and if it slips out, Lora, so help me heaven, I'll——'

'What does it matter?' Lora asked brutally. 'She's stopped writing—so I'm certainly not going after her. What good is a retired writer to an agent? The net result, my dear, is that you know *nothing* about this woman.'

'I suppose you're right,' Shelby admitted.

'Well, someone there has to know who she is. No one can keep that big a secret in a town that small.'

'But how do I find out?'

Lora drew on her cigarette. 'You're due for a vacation, aren't you?'

'Yes. I'm going up into New England next week.'

'No, you're not. You're going out to Warren's Grove and look for someone who isn't eating escargot.' She frowned. 'I must admit it would be easier if it was the other way round, but we have to take what we can get.'

'You're joking. It would be impossible!'

Lora shrugged. 'The alternative is to sit here and fret about whether she's going to pick up her mail. Besides, I just remembered where I heard about Warren's Grove.'

'Oh?'

'It might make it easier. And then again, it could be much, much harder.'

'Lora——'

'Warren's Grove is a mecca of sorts for writers. There's a sort of summer camp where the literary folk gather to inspire each other. I frown on that sort of thing, but at least one of my writers goes anyway.'

'What do you mean, at *least* one?'

'If the others go, they don't have the nerve to tell me,' Lora said. 'Mark might lend you a hand.'

'Who's Mark?'

'You have heard of Mark Buchanan?'

Shelby frowned. 'Is he the one who writes the abstract poetry?'

Lora sighed. 'God in heaven, Shelby, no. He's the political thriller. And I might add, quite good at it. I spent a month in Europe on my ten per cent of his last advance.'

Shelby whistled. 'If he's in that bracket, he probably won't want to bother with me.'

'Don't underestimate yourself, love. Or me. He owes me a favour. Besides, he might use it in a book himself someday—*The Search for Valerie St John*, or some such nonsense. I'll call him. Now get your New England reservations cancelled, and pack your bags!'

CHAPTER TWO

SHELBY opened her eyes and looked wearily out across the crisp fall landscape, where cornfields were turning golden brown as far as she could see. From the train window, she watched a car speeding along a highway that ran parallel to the tracks. The train's motion felt incredibly slow compared to the jet that had brought her from New York to Chicago; it felt as if they weren't getting anywhere at all, but Shelby saw that the car was slowly falling further and further behind.

It was not exactly the way she had planned to arrive in Warren's Grove, but it seemed that the major airlines refused to believe that there was any such town. The ticket clerk at O'Hare Airport had simply shaken her head when asked. The only air service was provided by a twin-engine commuter flight that made a dozen stops, she said, and besides that, the one plane of the day had already left. Better to be making progress than to waste a night in Chicago, Shelby thought, and so she bought a train ticket. At least this way she'd be in Warren's Grove by nightfall.

She watched the sun set over the rolling hills, and watched as the fading light caught against the trees and the wide fields. 'I thought the Midwest was supposed to be flat,' she mused.

She'd never been west of Chicago in her life, and she wasn't exactly looking forward to it now. A tour would have been one thing, or an honest-to-goodness vacation, but this crazy errand, looking for a woman she knew next to nothing about——

Why had she let Lora talk her into this, anyway? she wondered. She usually wasn't so easily pushed around, but this time she had let herself be bullied all the way to the airport.

She closed her eyes again and let herself drift back to early morning, in her apartment.

'Got your tickets?' Lora had demanded. 'All your luggage? Your credit cards?—though heaven knows if you can use them out on the frontier.'

'Come on, Lora, I'm not travelling by covered wagon, you know. And I'm not going out there for ever.'

Lora had shrugged, poured herself another cup of coffee, and said mildly, 'Then stop putting everything you own into that bag and come sit down.'

Shelby smiled a little. Lora was a good friend, and it must have been apparent that Shelby would need some bullying to get her on to that plane.

As a matter of fact, she thought, it wouldn't hurt to have someone bullying her right now. Here she was, little more than an hour from Warren's Grove, and she was daydreaming instead of doing her research.

She reached into the pocket of her carryall and pulled out the folder that she had sneaked out of the office on Friday. It contained the originals of all Valerie's letters, and that somewhere in there, if she only knew how to recognize them, lay the clues that could lead her to Valerie St John. Perhaps this thing wasn't so impossible after all, she thought, and for the first time she felt a glimmer of hope.

But the top sheet had nothing to do with Valerie, and she sat for a moment staring down at the crisp white of Lora's embossed stationery. 'It's Mark's phone number, and the address where he's staying,' Lora had said. 'I told him you were coming.'

'I'm sure he was thrilled,' Shelby had muttered.

'I also told him you're solving a mystery, it's the kind of thing he should really enjoy. Besides, he knows everybody in town. He's been going out there to that writers' camp for years.'

Well, Shelby told herself as she folded the stationery into a neat, sharp square, she'd call him. But she wouldn't count on his help. If Mark Buchanan wanted to join the search, she'd welcome all hands. And if he didn't . . .

She'd deal with that when she got to it, she decided, and tried to pretend that Mark Buchanan wouldn't be an asset after all. And then she turned her attention to Valerie's letters.

An hour later she pushed the folder back into the pocket of her bag and gathered her luggage together, scraps of Valerie's letters chasing each other around inside her head.

She totalled up the sum of her knowledge as she waited for the train to pull into the Warren's Grove station. She knew embarrassingly little about the woman she was searching for. Most of Valerie's letters concerned the work in progress, or Shelby. The woman had said almost nothing about herself, and she had done so in such a way that no one had really noticed how little they knew about Valerie St John.

I told her a lot more than she told me, Shelby thought. *If I'd only known how important it would be, I'd have pried a little harder.*

She had asked questions, of course, and hinted a few times that it really wasn't fair of Valerie not to add a few scraps of information. What were her hobbies, which authors did she like, did she have a family—all had resulted in tactful non-answers. The woman hadn't even been sporting enough to dedicate a book to anyone. That would at least have given Shelby another name to work from. And it would have been thoughtful of her to send a picture. *From now on*, Shelby decided, *I will demand a photograph of every author I work with!*

'Watch you step, ma'am.' The train attendant took her elbow to help her down from the car. Shelby stood on the platform and looked around, getting her first glimpse of Warren's Grove.

The air was crisp and cool as twilight nestled down over the rooftops. Up the street, Shelby could see lights on in the top storey of an office building that was about six floors tall. 'The Warren's Grove skyline at dusk,' she muttered, and stooped to pick up her luggage. 'Manhattan it ain't.'

There were a few people on the platform. Watching the train come through was probably the big entertainment of the evening, she thought. Then she saw the man who started towards her with what looked like recognition in his eyes. Tall, medium brown hair, shoulders that stooped a little—this must be Mark Buchanan.

He's not my idea of a man who writes political thrillers, Shelby told herself, *but who cares?* If Lora could, with a phone call from halfway across the country, produce results like this in a client, Shelby was all for it.

She gave him a warm, friendly smile, and was stunned when he looked coldly through her and walked on past. 'Hi, son,' he said, and put an arm around the shoulders of a teenaged boy who had got off the train right behind Shelby. 'How was Grandma?'

Shelby could have sunk into the asphalt sidewalk right there. *Listen, jerk*, she told herself. *Assuming that Mark Buchanan even cares that I'm coming, how in heaven's name could he have guessed that I'd be on that train? Lora didn't know it—I didn't even know it myself till I got to Chicago. How dumb can one woman be?*

'If he was such a good sleuth,' she muttered under her breath, 'he could have figured it out.'

And that made about as much sense as anything she'd considered all day, she realised.

'Ma'am?' The station agent had halted beside her. 'Did you speak to me?'

Shelby flushed crimson. Being caught talking to

herself was not a good way to start. 'No, I didn't, actually. But—where is there a hotel I could check into?'

'You're not being met? You might try the Warren House, just up the street.' He gestured. 'I'd send a redcap with you, but——' he shrugged '—as you can see, we don't have any at a depot this small. Take the luggage cart if you like. The bellboy will bring it back in the morning.'

Shelby's heart warmed a little. Small-town America might have its advantages after all, she concluded. She picked up her bags and started up the street.

The Warren House was a long Steamboat Gothic structure, built of old brick and trimmed in the finely worked white-painted gingerbread of another era. It rested on the riverbank as if it had stood there always, looking out across the silver ribbon of quiet water to the rolling plain beyond. A wide verandah ran along the whole front with a balcony opening off the second storey.

By the time she reached the wide front steps, Shelby's bags were getting heavy, and she was beginning to regret that she hadn't taken the station agent up on his offer to borrow a cart. But once inside the front doors, she forgot her tiredness.

The lobby of the Warren House was like a living room, with a small registration desk tucked into the curve of the oak staircase. A bright braided rug lay on the floor, and a fire snapped on the big stone hearth, dispelling the evening's chill. Furniture of no particular style was grouped casually around the fireplace, looking as if it had grown there over the years. Long windows, each glass panel etched with a huge 'W', looked out over the verandah.

A woman hurried from somewhere in the back, and greeted Shelby with a smile. 'Will you be checking in?'

'Yes. For about a week, if you can accommodate me.'

The woman laughed. 'Land, yes. It's off-season, now that the kids are back in school.' She looked down at the registration card. 'Breakfast is in the dining room any time from seven to ten—it's included with your room, and well worth coming down for, if I do say so myself. I hope you enjoy your stay with us, Miss Stuart. Are you on vacation?'

Shelby hesitated just a little. Might as well start now, she thought, and said, 'It's business, actually. I'm an editor, here to talk with one of my authors.'

'Now those we have plenty of—or did, up till Labour Day. Which one?'

'Valerie St John.' Then Shelby held her breath.

The woman repeated the name slowly, and then shook her head. 'That's one I've never heard of. What does she write?'

'Romance novels. That's her pen name, of course.' *Obviously I'm not lucky today*, Shelby told herself. She picked up her bags and turned towards the stairs. Then, suddenly, something that the woman had said registered. 'What did you say about Labour Day?' she asked.

'Oh, that's when the writers' camp closes. There's no heat out there, so everybody goes home when fall comes. If you'd come two weeks ago, you'd have had all kinds of authors to choose from.'

And that, Shelby thought bitterly, had probably been her best chance of finding Valerie. If anyone could find a writer, it was another writer ... Well, she still had Mark Buchanan to fall back on.

She climbed the stairs glumly and found her room. It was large and bright, with shuttered windows and a chandelier that had once been fuelled by gas. The starburst-patterned quilt on the four-poster bed had been made by hand, and on the night tables were crocheted doilies, starched and ruffled to perfection.

She tossed the key down on the table and picked up the telephone. She might as well not waste any time falling back on Mark Buchanan, she thought drily.

Seventeen rings later, she gave up. Apparently he wasn't the type to spend a Saturday night hanging around home waiting for a girl to call.

Or—horrible thought—had he gone home too, now that the camp had closed? Was Lora's information out of date?

Shelby stood in the shower for a long time, trying not to think. Then, in pyjamas and dressing gown, she curled up on the bed and made a list of her alternatives. At the bottom of the page, she wrote, 'Give up and go back to New York.'

She stared at it for a long time. Then she crossed it out with heavy black ink, turned the lamp off, and tried to go to sleep.

Breakfast was everything that had been promised. Fresh Danish, oozing strawberry jam. Blueberry muffins that were so hot they had to be handled with a fork. Link sausages with an aroma so compelling that it had awakened her. Coffee strong and hot from newly ground beans.

Finally she pushed her plate away, smiled at the little waitress who refilled her cup, and looked up to meet the eyes of the man she'd seen last night at the depot—the one who had been there to meet his son. Shelby started to blush just from the memory of the enticing smile she'd given him.

He said something to his companion at the table— Shelby could imagine what it was!—and the other man, who had been sitting with his back to her, turned to look Shelby over.

He made no effort to conceal his inspection. It was no casual glance over his shoulder; he had turned in his chair and rested an elbow on the back of it. He leaned back against the wall, his feet extended into the aisle, as if prepared to stay there all day and look.

Shelby bit her tongue and fought against the wave of colour that threatened to drown her. As coolly as she could, she returned his gaze. He would be tall, she thought, noting the length of his legs. He was obviously a workman; his arms and face were burned dark by the sun, his jeans were stained and spattered, and the cap that he'd tossed on to an adjoining table looked as if it had been used as a paintbrush. His pullover did nothing to hide the breadth of his shoulders and the powerful muscles of his upper arms.

He probably digs ditches for a living, Shelby thought, and has no better manners than to stare at every new girl in town . . .

Their eyes met and locked. Then he looked away; not in shame or embarrassment, she thought with surprise, but as if he'd seen all he wanted and was withdrawing from the staredown. He shifted in his chair and said something to his companion, who laughed.

Shelby pushed her cup of coffee away, untasted, and stalked out of the dining room. If the men in this town had no better manners than that, she raged to herself, a week here would be like running a perpetual gauntlet.

She retreated to her room and considered her list of leads. It was Sunday, so she couldn't go to the bank to ask if Valerie St John had an account there. She had a vague notion that they wouldn't tell her anyway, but perhaps she could work something out . . . The post office was closed, so there would be no one to check on the name of the person who had rented that box. The library might be open at weekends, though.

But first things had to come first. She got her jacket and Mark Buchanan's address, and started off down the main street. If he were still in town and had been out carousing last night, she thought, the chances were good that he'd be sleeping it off this morning.

The town was starting to come alive. Bells pealed from the steeple of the little white church, and people seemed to pour in from all directions. She stopped one man to ask directions, and then climbed on up the hill for another block towards the white house he had pointed out.

It was old, she saw as she came closer. The house was small and boxy, but on one corner it had a tower that must have a good view of the river. And swinging from the tower on a sort of scaffolding was a dark-haired man in a paint-spattered cap and jeans, wielding a brush against the wide clapboards—the man who had stared at her in the hotel dining room.

Shelby stopped at the foot of the tower. 'Hello up there,' she said, determined to be polite. He might have displayed no manners, but that was no excuse for her to do the same.

There was no answer.

'I'm looking for Mark Buchanan,' she called. She felt like a fool, shouting up at a man on a scaffold, her head tipped so far back that she could feel her neck muscles pulling.

There was a long silence. Then he called back, 'Why?'

'What business is it of yours?' Shelby snapped. Then she bit her tongue. 'I'm Shelby Stuart.'

This time, after a momentary pause, his head appeared over the corner of the scaffold. 'So what?' he said. 'You're also pretty dumb to stand right under a paint bucket like that.'

'Oh!' Shelby moved back a couple of yards, to the accompaniment of delighted laughter from above. It made her even madder. 'Would you be gentleman enough to tell me where to find Mr Buchanan?'

He looked as if he was thinking about it. 'No, I don't think I would,' he said. 'He's indisposed at the moment.'

'I suppose that means he's hung over!' At least, she thought, it meant that he was still in town.

The man nodded thoughtfully. 'Could be, I imagine,' he said. 'Why don't you come back next week?'

Shelby uttered a disgusted little moan, marched across the porch, and stabbed at the doorbell. She could hear the chimes inside, and she hoped cattily that it was reverberating through Mark Buchanan's head.

But there was no response. She rang the bell twice more before she gave up, and then she stepped off the porch and ran headlong into the painter.

She jumped and uttered a little scream. He set her back on her feet and said, 'Are you always this nervous?'

'Only when I have to deal with idiots,' she snapped. 'Please tell Mr Buchanan—whenever he comes to—that I'm staying at the Warren House and I'd really like to talk to him.'

'And what is this about?' He saw the startled expression in her eyes, and went on, 'If he owes you money or something——'

Up close, he was every inch as tall as she had calculated. He was also the owner of the most devastating set of curly eyelashes that Shelby had ever seen. Too bad they had to be wasted on a rube, she thought. 'Tell him it's about Valerie St John.'

'Ah, that figures. There's usually a woman in there somewhere. What is it this time?'

'Why don't you ask Mr Buchanan?' Shelby asked tartly.

'That wouldn't do me much good.' He knelt and opened a fresh gallon of paint. With it in one hand, he climbed back up the ladder to the makeshift scaffold. 'Who's Valerie St James?'

'John! St John!'

His face appeared over the edge of the scaffold. 'So I got the wrong apostle. Big deal. Who is she?'

'She's a romance writer.'

He was still for an instant. 'So that's what Lora was

blithering on about the other day,' he said thoughtfully. 'She can never remember that my answering service cuts people off after thirty seconds. I meant to call her back, but I hadn't got round to it yet.'

There was a long silence. Shelby wondered if she was going to faint. Then she swallowed hard and said, in a voice that trembled, '*You're* Mark Buchanan?'

'That's me. You'll be happy to note that I am not hung over after all. Just painting, which is trouble enough, I assure you.'

'I need your help,' she said.

'Ah, yes. To find the elusive Valerie St Something, who's hiding from you, the editor.' He appeared to consider it, and then shook his head. 'No thanks. If it comes right down to it in the battle of authors versus editors, I'm on her side.'

'Obviously Lora didn't tell you the whole story.'

He grinned. 'Lora wouldn't recognize a whole story if it was handed to her on a plate.' The first brushful of paint hit the clapboard with a swoosh.

Shelby was beginning to feel that the whole conversation was slipping from her control. 'Won't you help me?' she called, over the gentle slap-slap of the paintbrush.

'No. I don't think so. As far as I'm concerned the world has too many hack writers as it is—there's no need to help an editor locate another one. Let Valerie St Matthew-Mark-Luke-or-John—whichever she is—rest in peace.'

'But——' Shelby counted to ten and persisted, trying to sound reasonable, 'Won't you at least come down from there and talk about it? There's no need for the entire town to hear this conversation!'

'Why do we need to talk about it?' he asked politely. 'But if you insist on talking, you can come up if you like. Bring me that small brush, if you would, please—I need it up here in the corner.'

He hadn't even looked down. Shelby swore under her
breath and turned back towards the centre of town,
refusing to dignify this absurdity by arguing it out at
the top of her lungs.

'You might try the newspaper office!' he called after
her. 'The editor is sometimes there on Sundays!'

She didn't bother to acknowledge his comment. His
laughter haunted her all the way back to the hotel.

The newspaper office was locked, and so was the
library. She checked them both several times that
afternoon, and found no sign of life. Obviously, she
thought, the whole town of Warren's Grove took a
Sunday siesta.

Except, of course, for Mark Buchanan. Each time she
walked up the main street, she noted his progress. By
late afternoon he was no longer visible, and the whole
tower gleamed with a new coat of white.

Ultimately she gave up the search for the afternoon and
spent the rest of the day sitting in her hotel room, reading
Chamber of Commerce pamphlets about Warren's Grove
and dreaming up original ways to get even with one
smart-mouthed writer named Mark Buchanan.

She fell asleep there, and slept heavily for an hour.
When a knock at the door awakened her, it took an
instant for her to reorientate herself, and she was still
shaking herself awake when she answered the door.

Mark Buchanan was standing there. At least, she
amended sleepily, this man looked vaguely like Mark
Buchanan. But gone were the paint-spattered cap,
pullover, and jeans. This man wore cream-coloured
trousers and a dark brown linen jacket. His hair was
neatly combed, though still rebellious. And in his
hand—Shelby blinked and looked again.

'A daffodil?' she asked. Her voice was still hazy with
sleep. 'You're walking around this town carrying a
daffodil?'

'A peace offering,' he said, and handed it to her. 'Or are you a candy person instead?' He put a foil-wrapped chocolate-covered mint in her hand. 'Now will you forgive me?'

Shelby looked down at the delicate flower, and then up at him. He looked as woebegone as a scolded child, and she didn't believe for a minute that he meant it.

'You must have been hit by a steamroller this afternoon to change your attitude,' she said drily. She raised the daffodil to her nose, but there was no scent. Silk, she thought. He brought me a fake flower and a mint patty?

'In a manner of speaking I was,' he agreed, 'though I doubt that Lora would appreciate you calling her that. She told me I was an inconsiderate slob to you this morning and said that I should come and throw myself at your feet and beg forgiveness.'

'Lora always did have a way with words.'

'But I'd hate to test out the housecleaning that way. Would you mind awfully if I didn't kneel?'

'Frankly, I'd feel incredibly foolish if you did. Look, what do you want?'

'She told me all about your problem, and I'd like to enlist in the cause.'

'But you hate editors.'

He appeared to think that over. 'Well, yes,' he agreed finally, 'but Lora straightened me out on that. She said if you didn't find Valerie St Peter——'

'St John,' Shelby snapped.

'Whatever her name is. Anyway, Lora said that if you lost your job, you might end up as her secretary. And frankly, I don't want you muddling about with my manuscripts, so I want to keep you working for Jonas Brothers instead.'

She would have thrown him out, but she needed his help too badly.

'Why don't you put on something a little less

rumpled,' he suggested, 'and we'll plot our course of action over dinner?'

There were so many things she wanted to say that it would have taken Shelby all night to get through them. But she bit her tongue, shut the door in his face, and started to rummage through her wardrobe.

She'd show Mark Buchanan a thing or two, she fumed. He wouldn't continue to be so patronising for long.

CHAPTER THREE

MARK was talking to the hotel manager when Shelby came down the stairs. She felt vaguely like a teenager on her first date, and she was prepared to stand there unnoticed for half an hour while he finished his conversation. Instead she was mildly surprised when he looked up, came quickly across the room to meet her, and held the door for her. He seemed to have put on a new suit of manners along with his clean clothes, she thought.

'Why do you paint houses, anyway?' she asked.

He opened the passenger door of a moss-green sports car and smiled down at her as she got in. 'I don't, actually. Not houses, plural. That one belongs to my Aunt Pat, and she's touchy about who she lets work on it.'

'You amaze me,' Shelby said. 'She trusts you?'

He looked wounded. 'Actually,' he mused, and started the engine, 'it's a hobby. Some people use water colour on paper, others use oil on canvas. I do my best work with exterior latex on clapboards.'

'I wouldn't have thought that painting houses was your kind of thing.'

'Why not? Hasn't Lora told you all the ghastly details about me?'

I wish she had, Shelby thought. *I wish she had warned me.* 'No. But for someone who writes about intrigue and jewel thefts and international incidents——'

'I see. Unfortunately for the myth, I wouldn't know an international incident if one bit me. It's simply that I do my most creative thinking when my hands are busy.'

'Next you'll be telling me that you do needlepoint in the winter.'

He grinned. 'I haven't tried that yet. It doesn't sound like as much fun as playing tennis in Florida.' The car flashed past a rolling golf course and turned down a winding road. 'This golf course has the most difficult water hazard I've ever seen—the back nine runs right along the river. Are you a golfer?'

'Have a heart. In Manhattan? I've never had the opportunity.'

'Well, we can correct that in a hurry.'

'Thanks, but I'm here to work, remember? Do you live in Florida?'

'Occasionally. I vote in Connecticut, if that's what you're asking. But I spend summers out here——'

'Visiting Aunt Pat.'

He nodded. 'And hanging around the writers' camp to check out the competition.' He parked the car next to a low, rambling building.

'From what Lora says, you don't need to worry about the competition.'

'Writers always worry. If they don't, they start losing their edge.' He gestured. 'This is the Warren's Grove country club. As you will note, the clubhouse looks more like a converted drive-in restaurant. But despite appearances, they cook the best steaks in the state.'

The dining room was almost empty. The hostess, with a smile for Mark and a quizzical glance at Shelby, showed them to a corner table.

A couple at a nearby table waved, and the man called, 'Patricia's house is looking great, Mark.'

Mark bowed, with graceful elegance, and held Shelby's chair. 'Another couple of days should finish it.'

'Haven't seen her around for a while. Is she on vacation?'

'She's up north at the university, doing a workshop. She'll be back next week.'

The man laughed. 'That's the worst thing about teachers. Even when they retire, they never quit working.'

Mark turned back to Shelby. 'The worst part of a small town,' he said, 'is not that everyone knows all the gory details, it's that they really care.'

'That's why it should be no trick at all to find Valerie St John,' Shelby pointed out. 'It's just a matter of finding the person who knows.'

He nodded. 'That's right. If she's here in town, someone has to know.' He swirled his glass of wine and tasted it. 'Lora said the lady keeps her secrets. What do you have so far?'

'She worked in a library,' Shelby said. 'She mentioned that in a letter once.'

He frowned. 'Aunt Pat is on the library board. She could find out in a minute—if it was this library, of course.'

'That would be great!' Then Shelby's face fell. 'But if your aunt won't be back till next week—I have to leave Saturday, with or without Valerie St John.'

'When did you get into town, anyway?'

'Last night. And that reminds me—your famous answering service failed. I let your phone ring seventeen times, and I didn't even get a recording.'

Mark shrugged. 'I take Saturday nights off. You have high hopes, Shelby. One week isn't much time for a search like this.'

'I know.' It was soft, and held a note of fear. *If I don't find Valerie*, she was thinking, *I might as well not go back at all.*

There was a long silence. 'Well,' Mark said, 'there's no sense in giving up before we've even tried. Who knows? We might be lucky. Do you have any other personal details? How old is Valerie St Patrick's Day, anyway?'

'I don't know.'

Mark looked disgusted. 'Leave it to a woman. Any man would have found out by now. Do you mean that she could be anywhere between sixteen and sixty?'

'She's not a teenager,' Shelby disagreed. 'It's obvious that she has a great deal of experience with men, and her writing has tremendous depth and passion——'

Mark burst into laughter. A couple of minutes later, he recovered enough to say, 'There is no such thing as depth in that kind of trashy writing.'

Shelby would have liked to empty her wine glass over his head, but she maintained her dignity. 'You have probably never read a romance novel, Mark, so how do you know what you're talking about?'

'I have no respect for romances as a group, no,' he agreed. 'I do hope you aren't going to ask me to plough through Valerie's books so I'll know her better.'

Shelby, who had been thinking that very thing, stayed icily silent.

Mark, with a twinkle in his eyes, changed the subject.

She was halfway through her steak before she remembered that, angry as she was, she needed his help far more than he needed her. She forced herself to unbend. 'Valerie collects books,' she said finally.

'That's better than some writers I know. They collect bookies.' He pushed his plate away. 'That gets us a little further. Half the people in this town haven't read a book since they got out of school. The other half, because of the camp, are writing one. But not too many people actively collect them.'

'So how do we find out?' Shelby broke a warm dinner roll in half and buttered it.

He was sombre. 'You could pretend to be working for the fire inspector. Home libraries are a fire hazard, you know, because of all that paper. If you'd go around and knock on doors and ask how many books are kept there——'

'No, Mark.'

'A public opinion poll? No one would ever guess——'

'You don't have a very high opinion of the people in this town, do you?'

'On the contrary,' he retorted. 'One of the joys of living in a small town is being able to make fun of it. The trick is to laugh at yourself along with it. If an outsider were to say these things he'd be lynched, but when a native runs the place down, it gets chuckles.'

'Whatever you say,' Shelby murmured. 'Did you really grow up here?'

'Partly. Aunt Pat, who is my father's sister, didn't think I was being appropriately trained in the family traditions, so she started inviting me to spend summers with her when I was about six.'

'You couldn't be taught table manners in Connecticut?'

Mark smiled. 'Not to suit Aunt Pat. Patricia by name, and patrician by nature, that's Pat. It was a whole lot more than manners, though. My great-grandfather——' He paused, looking just a little puzzled. 'Or was it two greats? I can't remember. At any rate, we're descended from the Warren who started Warren's Grove. Aunt Pat has never let anyone forget her heritage.'

'Shall I kneel and kiss your ring?'

'Aunt Pat would probably consider it appropriate,' he agreed. 'She's very big on family trees and bloodlines and all that.'

'Are you also related to the presidential Buchanan?'

'I don't think so. Besides, according to Aunt Pat, they were mere upstarts—didn't get here till after the war. The Revolutionary War, that is.'

'I see.' Shelby was beginning to form a mental picture of the woman. She'd be an elderly, stout matron with blue hair, who always crooked her little finger when she was drinking tea, which would be served on the dot every afternoon . . .

'He built the house I'm painting,' Mark continued, 'the founding father, I mean. It's Aunt Pat's now, and she isn't about to let it fall down, either. In fact, she searched her soul for more than a year before she let them remodel the kitchen, but even Pat decided in the end that one must make some concessions to modern living.'

'I'm stunned.'

'You should well be,' he agreed solemnly. 'I think it was the cleaning woman who was responsible, actually.'

'For remodelling the kitchen?'

Mark nodded. 'She forced Aunt Pat into it by announcing that she refused to come back until the original linoleum had been removed. Pat hates to clean, so she had no choice. Good help is hard to get.'

'She must be a fascinating person.'

'The cleaning lady?'

'No. Aunt Pat.' This conversation, she thought, is beginning to sound crazy.

'I found the cleaning lady to be a much more original philosopher.' He refilled her wine glass. 'But you've distracted me, shame on you. Sitting here talking about Aunt Pat won't find Valerie St Thomas Acquinas.'

The correction—and a protest—trembled on Shelby's tongue, but she swallowed it.

'Where do we begin?' Mark asked. 'Shall we have lunch at the hotel tomorrow and then go to the library?'

'I was hoping to get a much earlier start,' Shelby pointed out.

'So who's stopping you? I have to paint some time. Of course, if you'd like to help me——'

'Thanks,' Shelby said politely. 'I think I'll check out the bank and the post office instead.'

'Whatever you like,' he said cheerfully. 'If you want to keep missing out on a great new hobby . . .'

The post office was small, with just one wall of the

glass-fronted lock boxes that allowed residents to pick up their mail at any hour. On Monday morning the lobby was busy, with people picking up the business mail that had accumulated over the weekend. There was a line at the service window, so Shelby wandered towards the mailboxes and ran her finger over the gold numbers till she found the one that belonged to Valerie St John.

It was empty, just as she had expected. Shelby hadn't written that last letter after all—the one that would have begged Valerie to reconsider her decision. She wondered, idly, whether it would have been waiting here or if it would have been picked up—and if so, by whom?

She stood there in the lobby for a long time, looking at each face as patrons came and went. Was this Valerie? Or this?

'May I help you, miss?'

She glanced around and realised that she was alone in the lobby. 'Yes,' she said, and her heart beat just a little faster. She pulled one of Valerie's pale pink envelopes out of her handbag and put it on the counter. 'Can you tell me who rents this post-office box?' she asked.

If she put her real name on it, she thought, her breath catching, then the search is over. I can just go out to the telephone booth in front, and call Valerie.

But Shelby was no fool. *If I were Valerie*, she thought, *and I was trying not to give myself away, would I be silly enough to put my real name on the box? Of course not. On the other hand, if everyone in town knows my name, would I dare to use anything else?*

The man behind the desk scratched his ear and turned towards the back room. 'Hey, Charlie,' he called. 'Somebody wants the name of a post-office box renter. Can I tell her?'

The answer came back with devastating clarity. 'Hell, no. It's confidential.'

Shelby was stunned. She had expected to be disappointed by the answer, but it had never occurred to her that she might get no answer at all.

The man turned back to Shelby, looking a little sorry, but firm. 'You've got a name there on the label, Miss,' he pointed out.

'But there might be a different name——'

He shook his head. 'Sorry, but I can't give out that information just to satisfy someone's curiosity. Now if there's been a crime committed, or something...'

Shelby shook her head. *Curiosity*, she thought bitterly. As though her motive were so light-hearted! But arguing with the post office would get her nowhere.

'Thanks,' she said, and put the envelope back in her handbag. *I wish I'd written that darned letter*, she thought. *By now Valerie might have picked up her mail.*

Shelby paused at the door and then turned back. At least she could put a message in that mailbox now, she decided, and maybe by tomorrow Valerie would have it.

It took just a minute to frame the few sentences that begged Valerie to call her at the hotel. Then she had to wait in line again at the service desk. 'Would you put this note in that box for me?' she asked, with her sweetest smile.

The clerk looked down at the folded sheet torn from Shelby's pocket diary, and then raised an eyebrow. 'Not without a stamp, I can't,' he said mildly.

'I don't even have an envelope,' she protested.

He reached into the supply drawer. 'Here you go. Put the address on it.'

Shelby, defeated, rummaged in her coin purse. 'It's a whole six feet over there,' she muttered. 'I should think it wouldn't need an address, much less a stamp!'

The clerk gave her a crooked grin. 'That's really first class service,' he pointed out.

Shelby swallowed her irritation. She should have expected it, she thought glumly, it was just her luck.

But she wouldn't be taken unawares at the bank, she decided, and spent the few minutes that it took her to walk there in dreaming up tricks to get the information she wanted.

The tall brick building was like something out of a movie—the kind of bank that one could imagine Jesse James riding up to with guns blazing. But inside, the bank was cool and quiet, with the same scent that identified banks throughout the civilised world.

When her turn came, Shelby stepped up to the teller with a brilliant smile and put a twenty-dollar bill on the marble counter. 'Valerie St John asked me to deposit this for her,' she said. 'I'm sorry I don't know the account number.' Then she waited, trying not to hold her breath.

The teller sounded bored. 'Checking or savings account?' she asked, reaching for the bill.

Shelby did her best to look like a dizzy blonde. 'I don't remember if she even told me,' she said, and thought, *Jackpot! Valerie has an account!*

'I'll have to check,' the teller said. 'It'll take a while to find the account number.'

Shelby smiled. 'I'll wait,' she assured the girl.

It took what felt like for ever. Ten minutes into the wait, Shelby was ready to give up. There might be no account after all, she told herself; the teller had simply assumed that Shelby knew what she was talking about.

The teller came back with a slip of paper. 'I can't find any record——'

Shelby's heart sank.

'Of a checking account,' the girl went on. 'I'll put this in savings for her, but you might ask to be sure that was what she wanted done.' Her hands were busy as she spoke.

And there goes my twenty dollars, Shelby thought. Ah, well, she told herself philosophically, it was spent in a good cause.

Her fingers itched to seize the slip of paper that the girl held. On that tiny scrap, Shelby was certain, was Valerie St John's real name. After all, bank accounts couldn't blithely be started in random names. Someone at the bank had to know who Valerie really was . . .

She stood on the steps of the bank and glanced at her watch. She had time for one more stop before meeting Mark for lunch—should it be the newspaper office or the library?

She'd leave the library till later; Mark, because of his aunt's position, might be better able to get information. But a search of the newspaper's clipping files might turn up the answer. If Valerie had slipped up on her anonymity even once in a town this size, the newspaper might have mentioned it.

She glanced up the hill where the fresh paint on the tower of Patricia Buchanan's house gleamed in the sunlight. Now that the tower was done, she couldn't see where Mark was working. She wished that he was with her.

The scent of ink hung like a cloud in the small storefront printing plant, tickling Shelby's nose till she wanted to sneeze. The front office, which was half do-it-yourself ad agency and half office supply store, was dimly lit and dusty. Shelby picked up a couple of legal pads and a new pen.

A short woman wearing very red lipstick bustled up with a smile. It's probably the first sale she's made in a week, Shelby thought with another glance around the shop.

'I'm looking for information on a resident of Warren's Grove,' she told the woman. 'Do you keep clipping files?'

'A morgue, you mean?' The woman handed Shelby her change and put her purchases in a bag. 'Not really. We keep all the old issues, of course—they're bound by the year. When would this have been?'

Shelby could have sat down in the middle of the floor and cried. She wanted to scream, what kind of newspaper doesn't clip its major stories and file them by subject?

'I don't have a date.' But her brain was calculating feverishly. Valerie's first book had landed on Shelby's desk three years before. She must have been writing before that; in fact, a news story might have been more likely before Valerie achieved any kind of success and decided to remain an unknown. 'It could have been any time in the past five years,' she said glumly.

'I can get the bound volumes for you,' the woman offered. 'Or even better, the library has all the old issues on microfilm. It's easier to use that way.'

Everything kept leading back to the library, Shelby thought. She could feel a headache starting already, just behind her left ear, as she thought about reading five years' worth of microfilm, looking for a story that might be anywhere—in the personal columns, in the society notes—or nowhere at all. It would take days, and then she would never be sure that she hadn't missed something.

'Thanks, anyway,' she said, and started towards the hotel, hoping that Mark might have some better ideas. Obviously, Shelby thought, she herself was a loss when it came to sleuthing.

She was drinking coffee and was almost ready to give up on him when he finally appeared. His hair was still damp from a shower, and he had changed from painting clothes to clean jeans. His brightly-printed shirt was buttoned only halfway up, and the sleeves were rolled to the elbow.

Shelby looked up the instant that he appeared, as if some magnet had drawn her eyes to him.

No wonder he was one of Lora's favourites, she thought, noting the tanned chest covered with curly dark hair, Lora like men who were men. And how stupid it was, Shelby told herself roundly, to feel a stab of jealousy towards Lora.

Then she told herself crossly that it wasn't jealousy; it was good, old-fashioned irritation at a guy who thought he was Prince Charming. 'You're late,' she accused.

'Sorry.' He didn't sound it. 'The painting didn't go well at all today. I hope the search was more successful.'

'Not so you'd notice. I already ordered, by the way.'

He smiled at the waitress, who looked as though she'd like to throw herself into his lap, and told her to bring him a cheeseburger and fries.

I wish the girl would get down to business, Shelby thought. Why didn't Lora warn her that every woman within ten miles thought this guy was the answer to her prayers?

'No luck?' he asked sympathetically.

She shook her head. 'I struck out at the post office and the newspaper. I did a little better at the bank, but it cost me twenty dollars to find out that Valerie St John has a savings account.'

He looked horrified. 'You bribed a bank teller?'

'No, I didn't! And stop shouting, please.' Shelby told him the details of her morning, and was a little surprised when he laughed.

'You learn fast, don't you, Shelby?' he said.

The gleam of humour in his dark eyes made her breathing do funny things. So this was how the waitress felt, she thought a little bemusedly. That smile could melt stone.

Mark attacked his cheeseburger as if he were starving. 'So what do we do this afternoon?'

'The library. Can you convince them to tell you, if they know anything?'

'I can only try. There's a woman in the research department . . .'

Shelby wasn't surprised. 'Then let's get started.'

'Shelby, I've been doing physical work all morning, and I'm hungry. The peach pie is great here.'

'No thanks.'

She waited impatiently, fidgeting with her club sandwich, while he polished off pie and ice cream. But finally he was ready to go.

'If you can stand going to the post office again, I have to pick up Aunt Pat's mail,' he told her. 'Then I'm all yours for the rest of the afternoon.'

Shelby almost said, 'Save that line for the waitress,' but she caught herself. He probably didn't even realise what he'd said. 'We've got time.'

Patricia Buchanan's post-office box was one of the oldest set, at the opposite end of the wall from Valerie St John's. 'Did she inherit that from the original Warren, too?' Shelby asked. 'Box number one, for heaven's sake!'

Mark looked intrigued. 'I don't know, I'll have to ask her.' He flipped through the envelopes and stopped at a pink slip of paper. 'There's a package too big to fit in the box,' he said. 'I'll have to wait in line. Is that the famous PO box?'

Shelby was staring at her note in Valerie's mailbox, as if by concentration she could make its owner come in to retrieve it.

'I see she has a message,' Mark said. 'Can you read the return address through the glass?'

'I don't need to. I am the return address.' Shelby kept staring.

'What an original idea! Don't leave noseprints on the door,' Mark recommended, and went to stand in line to get Pat's package.

Shelby looked up a few minutes later and saw him huddled in a corner with a short, greying man whose necktie was loose. In another five minutes, he was back.

'Friend of yours?' she asked.

'In a manner of speaking. That's the postmaster. The name on the box is——'

Shelby seized his arm. 'You did it?' she whispered unbelievingly.

'Valerie St John. Sorry, Shelby. It's the only name on the papers.'

'Is that legal?' Shelby complained. 'I mean, using an alias——'

Mark shrugged. 'Who cares if it's legal? She did it.'

'I can't believe that the post office would allow someone to use a phoney name——'

'Maybe they didn't know it was phoney.'

'In a town this size? Come on, Mark! You're the one who told me that everyone knows everyone!'

'At any rate, if you want her to come back to work for you,' he said firmly, 'I wouldn't report her to Uncle Sam for using an alias to get her mail. She might not appreciate the hornet's nest that you would be stirring up.'

Shelby had to admit the wisdom of that. It wasn't that she wanted to cause trouble, she told herself, but it was horribly frustrating to be so very close to Valerie St John and not be able to reach her.

'So you stopped at the newspaper office and Jake didn't remember printing anything about Valerie?' Mark mused.

'Jake? Who's he? I just talked to the woman in the front office. I told you that they don't keep clipping files.'

Mark smiled as if she'd said something brilliant. 'It's careless, I admit, but they do have records—every story that paper has run in ten years is filed neatly away in Jake Baxter's head. He's the editor.'

'It might be easier than microfilm,' Shelby admitted.

'Sure, it's easier. Jake has total recall—it's better than an index. Let's go talk to him.'

'But the library—everything points back there!'

'Twenty minutes with Jake and we'll be on our way. Either you'll have Valerie's home phone number or you'll know that Jake never heard of her either. And if I was betting——'

Shelby wavered. 'But——'

'Look, do you want my help and advice or not?'

She hadn't done at all well that morning without it, she reminded herself. 'If you insist, we'll go to the newspaper office first.'

He rewarded her with a smile. 'That's my girl.'

They found the editor in his office, feet propped up on his desk, green eyeshade cocked at an angle.

Shelby, who hadn't known that they still made such headgear, occupied herself with a study of it while Mark explained their problem. Then the editor's keen blue eyes shifted to her.

'Nope,' he said. 'Fact is, Miss Stuart, we steer clear of all those writers. Too darn many of them, and the envy that runs through that camp——! I published a story one of them did for me five years ago, and then they all wanted space for their pet projects. Well, you know how it is, being an editor.'

Shelby nodded.

'Now Mark here is on the other side of the fence,' Jake chuckled.

'Are you going to tell me again that editors and writers are natural enemies?' Mark asked.

'Well, you're an exception to your kind,' Jake said. 'A writer who isn't stuck on every word that flows through his mind is a rarity.'

'But about Valerie——' Shelby prompted.

'Never heard of her.'

'How about women around town who write?' Mark prompted. 'Is there anyone at all who might be Valerie in hiding?'

'Tell you the truth, I avoid all writers except my own. We ran that story on you, Mark, when your first book came out, and we have to do the duty stories when somebody prints up the family tree. I wish Patricia hadn't started that fad around here,' he complained. 'It's gone crazy.'

'But no Valerie,' Shelby murmured.

'Nobody. Tell me about yourself, Miss Stuart. What brings a high-powered New York editor out here to look for Valerie St John? Is she that good?'

Shelby ran through the truth in her mind, rearranging and discarding, deciding what was appropriate for public knowledge. 'She's very good indeed. I want to talk to her about her next book.'

Jake chuckled. 'But she hasn't ever given you her real name?'

'That's right.'

'I'll see what I can find out. In the meantime, you're a bit of a celebrity yourself, you know. Something unusual for Warren's Grove, to have an editor here instead of all those writers. May I just snap a picture of you?'

'Why not?' Shelby said. It was nice to know that she would make this nice old man's file of memories.

While the editor manoeuvred for the best angle, Mark said, 'If you hear anything, Jake——'

'Oh, I'll find you up at Patricia's, or Miss Stuart down at the hotel. Nice to meet you, miss.'

The woman who tended the front office was beside the door, on tiptoe, looking as if she was trying to float. 'You know Valerie St John?' she asked Shelby.

'I edit her books,' Shelby said. 'But as far as knowing her——'

The woman's face was glowing. 'She's my favourite author,' she bubbled. 'I read all her books. I can't believe that Valerie St John lives right here in Warren's Grove, and nobody even knew it! Just wait till I tell the ladies in my bridge club!'

CHAPTER FOUR

THEY walked towards the library in total silence, and it wasn't till they had reached the stone steps at the front entrance of the small brick building that Shelby said, 'Why do I feel as if I've been riding a tornado and I just lost control?'

There was a brief hesitation, then Mark said, 'Because you have excellent instincts, my dear. That woman is the biggest gossip in town. Jake only keeps her because she knows everyone's business.'

'She wasn't kidding about telling her friends?'

'Oh, the bridge club will know every gory detail by tomorrow morning, I'd say.' He paused. 'Let me qualify that. That's if she has a busy day and can't spend much time on the phone. Otherwise they'll know tonight.'

Shelby sighed. 'I suppose it might work out for the best. If enough people know, the word is bound to reach Valerie—wherever she is.'

Mark gave her an inquiring look. 'I don't think you'll have trouble with enough people knowing,' he drawled.

'Shhh!' said the woman behind the desk. She was checking out a stack of books to a child who was barely tall enough to see over the edge. Then she looked up. 'Oh, it's you, Mr Buchanan.'

'Hello, Miss Branch. This is Shelby Stuart. She's looking for an author who lives here in town.'

The woman's eyes brightened. 'Oh, we have several authors besides Mr Buchanan, who is our most famous, of course. What's the name?'

Shelby took a deep breath and embarked on her story one more time. 'Her pen name is Valerie St John.'

The librarian repeated it thoughtfully and shook her head. 'What does she write?'

'Romances. I'm her editor at Jonas Brothers.'

'Oh. Those.' The librarian's tone left no doubt as to her opinion of Valerie's choice of topic.

Mark stifled a laugh. Shelby glared at him and wished that she had the nerve to grab the nearest book cart and drive it over his toes.

'That kind of book is in the rack over there.' The librarian pointed. 'As for finding out who she really is, I'm afraid I couldn't be of any help.'

'Do you have any sort of listing of local writers?' Shelby begged. At this point, she would have grabbed at any chance.

'We have a local history room, and we do collect the works of all residents. But I can tell you this much— there's certainly nothing in there by Valerie St John.'

'Do you have any of her books?'

'Of course.' The librarian sniffed. 'I can't understand, myself, why that sort of thing is so popular. But we keep them, if only because some women start by reading them and then go on to better literature.'

'Mind if we just look around?' Mark asked.

'Not at all. That's what the library is for,' the woman said coolly.

Shelby hung back. 'Just one more question,' she said. 'Valerie told me that she worked in a library for a time. Does anyone on your staff write?'

The librarian drew herself up to her full height. 'No one on our staff would consider such stuff *writing*,' she sniffed.

'As for that,' Shelby said sweetly, 'it pays rather well. Perhaps she isn't on the staff any more.'

Mark grabbed her arm and whisked her off to the romance shelves. 'What are you, some kind of nut?' he asked. 'You can't talk that way to her!'

'I just did,' Shelby pointed out resentfully. 'If you

were writing a romance, would you tell that old battleaxe about it? Of course not—and I'll bet Valerie didn't either. So there!'

Several hundred battered paperback books filled the rack that the librarian had pointed out. Shelby ran a hand across them. Five years in the business, and the finished product could still give her a sense of pride, of delight. *If I lose my job*, she thought drearily, *I don't know what I'll do.*

'I'll bet anything,' she said thoughtfully, 'that if we could find out who quit working here within the last three years, we'd have Valerie.'

'Well, you won't find out by talking that way to the chief librarian. For heaven's sake, Shelby, don't you have any tact?'

'Not when people call my hard work trash, no.'

He picked up a book. 'So this is a sample of Valerie St John the Divine's work?'

Shelby glanced at the title. 'That was her first one. She wasn't about to give us any help, was she?'

'Miss Branch? Surely you're not surprised. Now that you've made her mad, you'll have to wait for Aunt Pat to get home,' he pointed out. 'She can probably recite the list of who worked here and when—and why they left.'

'And I won't be here,' Shelby muttered. She was beginning to regret her quick tongue. It wasn't the first time it had got her into trouble.

'You could always stay longer.'

'Can't. I'm only getting a week's vacation this fall.' Then she added stoutly, 'What's wrong with pure entertainment, anyway? Why does something have to be literary to have merit? If they applied that standard to movies and television, there wouldn't be anything to watch.'

'True enough,' Mark murmured.

Shelby was warming to her topic. 'She needn't treat romances as if they're pornographic.'

'Aren't they?'

'Dammit, no!'

'Shhh,' said a voice from the front desk.

'Look,' Mark said, tucking Valerie's book under his elbow, 'let's get out of here before she takes my library card out of the file and burns it for daring to bring you in—you rabble-rouser.'

'I'm sorry.'

'No, you're not. I'll never be brave enough to show my face in here again.'

He stopped at the desk and dropped the book on it. 'Doing my research,' he explained when the librarian looked at the title and turned up her nose.

'It hardly seems your kind of reading, Mr Buchanan,' she said tartly. She wrote his name on the card. 'It'll be due in two weeks—though I don't doubt that you could read it in a couple of hours.'

Mark grinned. 'If I can stand to sit through it all at once,' he taunted in a confidential whisper, with a glance at Shelby.

But Shelby didn't rise to the bait. She was paying no attention to him; she was staring at the book card in the librarian's hand.

'Let's go, Shelby.'

Shelby followed him reluctantly to the door, and then stopped dead. 'Wait, Mark,' she whispered. 'That card—she wrote your name on it when she checked out the book.'

'Yeah. Mark Buchanan—that's me. Why?'

'Why didn't she use your number? You said you have one——'

'Because it's quicker to jot down the name. Why?'

Shelby stared thoughtfully through the bevelled glass door, but she didn't see the town square beyond. Her brain was working furiously. 'Does she do that all the time?'

'Unless someone has a lot of books. Then she looks

up the card and uses the number because it's shorter. Why are you asking me all this stuff, Shel?'

'Because——' Shelby's eyes were starry. 'There are certain subjects in Valerie's books that she has done a great deal of research on. If she checked out the books here, then——' She paused.

Mark's puzzlement dropped from his face. 'Then her name might be on the card!'

'And it would have to be her real name,' Shelby pointed out. 'The post office and the bank might not question an alias, but the tyrant at that desk probably insists on seeing a birth certificate before she issues a library card.'

Mark grinned. 'That's just about the truth,' he admitted. 'Where do we begin?'

Two hours later the librarian decreed that it was closing time and kicked them out. Shelby stuffed the sheaf of paper covered with names into her handbag to avoid Miss Branch's suspicious eyes, and walked out with her head high. 'You'd have thought from the way she acted that we were back in the corner writing naughty words in the books,' she sniffed as they walked back towards the hotel.

'I doubt it,' Mark said comfortably. 'I don't think she believes that you can even spell.' He stretched. 'That's one of the harder afternoons of research I've ever done—like hunting a needle in a haystack. Let's adjourn somewhere for attitude adjustment hour.'

'What does that mean?' The September air was crisp and fresh. Somewhere a pile of leaves was burning, and the scent teased Shelby's nose.

'In other words—I would like a stiff drink. Is the Sand Bar in the hotel all right with you?'

'Sure.' Shelby was skimming the list of names. 'I think if we recopy all of these——'

Mark groaned. 'You wrote them once. Isn't that enough?'

Shelby ignored the protest. 'We can eliminate the ones that only turn up once. But if one person has checked out books in all of those areas——'

'Then we might have Valerie in our ingenious little net. Did you know there's a state law against this, by the way? Library information is supposed to be confidential.'

'So are post-office box holders, but you got that one,' Shelby answered sweetly.

'All right. I give up. But you have to buy me a Scotch and water first—then I'll go back to work.'

He filched the corner booth in The Sand Bar from a couple who had hesitated an instant too long in the doorway. Shelby giggled. 'You're devious, Mark,' she accused.

'That's nothing new. Aunt Pat has been telling me that for decades.' His smile had the predictable effect on the waitress. For once, Shelby didn't mind; it got her glass of wine on to the table much faster. She took a long, grateful swallow.

'I could have told you that this kind of thing is dry work,' Mark said. 'I remember when I was writing about a jewel theft in Barcelona. The thieves fled to Budapest——'

'You're joking.'

'Not at all.' He sounded hurt.

'Why Budapest?'

'It made sense at the time. At any rate, you have no idea how hard it is to find out the minute details of everyday life in Budapest. Just as soon as you take a chance on something, a reader catches you out.'

'I get it. If you write that the cathedral bells rang out at noon——'

'Then some nitpicking reader informs you that there are no bells in the cathedral——'

'Or that they don't ring at noon——'

He nodded. 'Or that there's no cathedral at all. You

get the idea. The point is, you have to know a certain amount in order to be able to ask the right questions. I just hope you know enough about Valerie St John to know what she needed to research.'

'I think I do. She'd mention what she was working on sometimes in the letters. If it was important enough to mention, it must have been giving her trouble.'

'I still think that checking the travel books would have made more sense.' He reached for her list. 'Reading up on African art I can understand—it's a rare bird in Warren's Grove who practices that hobby. But gourmet cooking?'

'She doesn't like it. Therefore, she isn't likely to own any gourmet cookbooks, and not everyone knows the difference between bouillabaisse and boeuf bourguignon. That one she had to look up.'

'So would I,' Mark pointed out. 'Have to look it up, that is. If, of course, I ever needed to know it—which I can't imagine.'

'Yes, I noticed that you ordered a cheeseburger for lunch,' Shelby said tartly. 'What do you eat at a good restaurant?'

Mark grinned. 'I ask the waiter to bring me the closest thing to a steak that he has. It's only failed a couple of times.' He looked thoughtful. 'Of course, both of those were colossal failures.'

'You should expand your horizons.'

'Why?' he asked reasonably. 'And if you tell me that you really enjoy snails broiled in butter, or whatever those barbarians do to them——'

Shelby tried to look outraged, but she ended up bursting into giggles. 'All right, I admit that I draw the line at snails. At least as a regular diet.'

'Good. Because I not only refuse to eat them, I will absolutely not watch while someone else does. Shall we have another drink, or are you ready to go somewhere and get another cheeseburger?'

'One glass of wine is plenty, thanks. But I'm not ready for dinner—it's early.'

'City girl,' Mark grumbled. 'In that case, why don't you show me Valerie's letters? Maybe I can find something in them that you aren't seeing.'

'Good point. I've read them so many times I can practically recite them.' She led the way up to her room. Once inside, she took the folder of letters from the night table drawer and handed it to Mark. He tossed himself down on the bed and picked up the top sheet.

'Pink stationery?' he said doubtfully.

'Have you no imagination? It's for romance—of course.' She sat quietly in the rocking chair and began to organise the list of names while he read the letters. Finally he slid the pile back into the folder and laid it aside.

'Quite a woman,' he said. 'Doesn't give away much of anything, does she?'

'No, she doesn't.' There was a long silence. 'You know,' Shelby said, a little shyly, 'I really do hope that we find Valerie. It's more than just talking to her about writing another book. It sounds silly, I know——'

He raised an eyebrow.

'But I feel that she's my friend,' Shelby blurted in a rush of words. 'After writing to her for almost three years, losing her is a blow. Whether she ever writes a book for me again isn't the point.' Then she stared at the braided oval rug on the floor, feeling as if she had bared her soul to this man who would probably think her foolish.

The bed creaked as he rolled off it. He came to stand beside her chair, but Shelby didn't look up. She was too afraid of what she might see in those devilishly dark eyes.

'I hope you find her, too,' Mark said, very softly.

Shelby looked up, surprised by the tone of his voice. His arm slipped around her shoulders, and he kissed her. It was almost a brotherly kiss, she thought, gentle and sweet and tender. His cologne seemed to be a blanket around her, its scent soothing and comforting and soft.

'Why did you do that?' she asked, as he stood up straight again.

'Because you looked as if you were about to cry,' he said. 'I thought if you slapped me it would make you forget your troubles.'

She thought about that for a moment. 'But I didn't want to slap you,' she murmured.

He smiled, slowly. 'I know.'

Shelby pulled her feet up under her and clasped her arms around her knees. 'Why am I sitting out here before the crack of dawn watching you paint?' she asked plaintively.

Mark took a quick look at the sky. 'I beg to differ with you, Shelby,' he said. 'Dawn has not only cracked, it is entirely shattered. I told you that I do my best creative thinking while my hands are busy. If you'd like to try it, there's another brush over there.'

'No, thanks. I do my best work when I'm half-asleep.'

'In that case it should be a very productive day.' His tone was dry.

He had knocked on her door so early that Shelby had thought for a while that she was having a nightmare, and insisted that she come with him. Her first thought had been that he'd discovered Valerie overnight and wanted to surprise her, and when she had found herself sitting instead on a tarpaulin beside Patricia Buchanan's almost-white house, she had been ready to pour a gallon of paint over him.

Mark worked silently for another hour. Finally, out of boredom, Shelby went around the corner and started pulling loose paint off the boards.

If I were still in New York, she thought, *I'd be just settling down at my desk with a pile of manuscripts and a fresh cup of coffee, and I'd be ready for a long, leisurely day of enjoyable reading . . .*

Interrupted, she added to herself, by at least seventy phone calls, a dozen conferences with the other editors, and her secretary wanting to know when she was planning to answer all these letters that were stacked up on the desk. And at the end of the day, Shelby reminded herself, she would look at that little pile of manila envelopes and wonder how she could accomplish so little when she'd been there for so many hours . . .

Then, from the top of the ladder came a shout that made her jump and ram her hand against the house.

'What?' she said crossly, examining her skinned knuckles.

'I've got it!'

'You know where to find Valerie?' She dashed around the corner and looked up at him eagerly.

'Oh—I'd forgotten about Valerie. I've been thinking about a new idea for a book.'

'Great,' Shelby muttered.

'If romances are so easy to write——'

'I never said they were.'

'So let's not argue about unimportant things. I'll give you the idea free. If you lose your job, you can cross the fence and become a writer instead.'

'I don't want to write the things, I just want——'

Mark ignored the interruption. 'It's about an interior decorator who falls in love with a house painter named Chip.'

'That's not a romantic name.' Then she saw the pun, and groaned.

Mark grinned down at her. 'Chip tries to brush her off, but she keeps getting into scrapes that he has to rescue her from——'

'Chip? Brush? Scrapes?' Shelby sat down on the tarpaulin again. This time she was tempted to put her hands over her ears. 'What a stirring experience it must have been for you to think of all that.'

He rewarded her with a smile. 'See? When you wake up, you're fun to be around.'

'What about Valerie?'

'I have no idea if she's fun.'

Shelby counted to ten. 'I meant, do you have any brilliant ideas this morning for finding her? Why did you drag me out here, anyway?'

'So we could brainstorm.'

'Silently?' Shelby asked tartly.

'It's not my fault you can't talk in the morning. Let's check all of the bookstores today.'

'Warren's Grove has more than one?'

'Well—if you count the newsstand at the all-night drug store, yes. And speaking of books, that autograph idea is really neat.'

Shelby was only half listening. 'You lost me. What do you mean?'

'Printing the author's signature on the title page. I didn't see that till last night, when I was using Valerie's magnum opus to read myself to sleep. She did it in less than a chapter, too. I want to tell you, the girl shows wonderful promise in the sleeping pill market——'

'Hold it!' Shelby ordered. 'Back up. What do you mean, author's signature?'

Mark sighed. 'Don't you speak English?'

'But we don't print the author's signature.' She stared up at him for a moment, and then she leaped to her feet. 'Mark, *was that book autographed*?'

'Don't shout at me,' he complained. 'It certainly has Valerie's name on it.'

'Where is it?'

Mark turned around precariously on the ladder. 'On

the title page, I told you. I haven't seen this much action from you in two days.'

'Not the signature, dummy—the book! Where did you leave the book?'

'On the nightstand in my bedroom. The one at the top of the back stairs.'

Shelby was already through the back door. She wasted half a moment appreciating Patricia Buchanan's elegant country kitchen and then flew up the narrow, winding stairs.

The bedroom at the top was large and airy, much larger than she would have expected from seeing the exterior of the house. But it was obviously a guest room, with few signs that it was even in use. The bed belonged in a museum, the headboard was scrolled and curved like an old-fashioned horsedrawn sleigh. She sat down on the edge of the bed and reached with trembling hands for the paperback that lay on the night table.

The signature was real. There was no doubt about that—Valerie's spiky handwriting was too familiar for Shelby to mistake it.

'It's been a while since she signed it,' she said as Mark came into the room. 'Look, there's a stain where some fool set a glass down and smeared the ink.'

'Don't look at me!' he said defensively. 'Aunt Pat taught me never to abuse books—even trashy ones. Do you mean that really is an autograph?'

'Oh, yes. It's her signature.' Shelby sighed. 'It's a little comfort—at least I know she's here. But when would she have done it? It can't have been too long, or the librarian would have noticed.'

Mark nodded. 'She would consider it to be defacing public property,' he agreed, 'unless she assumed as I did that it was supposed to be part of the book. But really, Shelby—can you imagine Miss Branch spending her time inspecting that shelf to be sure the romances are all in good shape?'

Shelby had to smile at that. 'She probably goes to great effort to avoid that rack,' she agreed. 'So you think it could have been signed at any time?'

'Much as I hate to admit it—yes. I'll take my life into my hands and ask Miss Branch when that book was checked out last, but don't get your hopes up. I glanced at the card when she checked it out, and I think it was weeks ago.'

Shelby sighed. 'Can I at least go along when you ask her?'

'Only if you promise to let me do the talking this time,' Mark threatened. 'I forgot to tell you—there's a young woman outside waiting to see you. She has a package.'

'I'm not expecting anything,' Shelby said, startled.

Mark grinned. 'You really have no idea what you've turned loose, do you?' he said cryptically, and led the way down the stairs.

The woman was very young, very blonde, and very nervous. She was wearing vivid purple eyeshadow and approximately a ton of eyeliner. The package she was clutching was a pocket folder, stuffed to bursting with notebook paper. It didn't take an expert to diagnose that she was a frustrated writer with an orphaned manuscript.

'Dammit, Mark,' Shelby hissed, 'why didn't you tell her I was too busy to see her?'

'Because,' he hissed back, 'by lunchtime the whole town would have heard that you were busy in my bed.'

'So who cares what the town hears?'

'Valerie might have a morality hangup.'

Shelby laughed. 'It's apparent that you didn't get very far into that book last night, if you think Valerie is a prude!'

His smile was angelic. 'I thought you said romances weren't pornographic.'

Shelby gave it up as a hopeless cause and went to greet the young woman. 'May I help you?'

'Miss Stuart? Are you really a book editor?'

Shelby sighed. 'That's right.'

'Well, I wrote a book, and——' she shoved the folder into Shelby's arms with a strength that would have done credit to a prize fighter, 'here it is.'

And what am I supposed to do with it? Shelby wondered. *Use it as kindling for my next bonfire, which is probably what it's worth?*

'Will you read it?' The girl's eyes, under the coats of makeup, were like those of a homeless puppy.

'I—I'm very busy, actually——' The girl's eyes saddened, and Shelby melted. 'Sure. Why not? I'll leave it for you at the hotel desk when I've finished.'

'Oh, that's wonderful! And just one more thing——'

Here it comes, Shelby thought.

'Would you autograph this for me?' The girl whipped a newspaper out of her totebag.

Why on earth, Shelby wondered. Then she saw the headline that stretched the width of the front page. VALERIE ST JOHN, WHO ARE YOU? it screamed in letters two inches tall. And below it was the picture that the editor had taken of Shelby in his office.

'Mark! Look what your friend Jake did to me!' she yelled.

He had climbed the ladder again, but he came down in a hurry and took the paper out of her shaking hands. 'Come on, Shelby, what did you expect?'

'I didn't expect the top of the front page, headlines that make it look like a murder, and a picture of me that looks fifteen pounds overweight and forty years old——'

'Ah, it's the picture that upset you,' Mark said sagely. 'You're right, it isn't flattering. Jake needs to improve his camera technique.'

Shelby was speechless with rage.

'Shel, stop screeching,' he recommended. 'For a New York girl, you're awfully naive. When a newspaperman asks for your picture, it usually isn't because he wants to carry it around in his locket.' He handed the newspaper back and and climbed the ladder again. 'Think positive,' he called down. 'Everyone within fifty miles now knows you're looking for Valerie.'

Shelby scrawled her name across the story and gave it to the girl. Then, offended, she sat down crosslegged on the tarpaulin and maintained absolute silence for the next hour, just to show Mark Buchanan.

It didn't work. He whistled while he worked, sang a snatch of a popular tune now and then, occasionally dropped a new idea for his book about the house painter. 'Chip owns a couple of dogs,' he told her once. 'One's named Spot and the other Patch——'

That was when Shelby rose, with dignity. 'Let me know what you find out at the library,' she said coldly. 'I'll check the bookstores. Have a good day.'

The bookstore managers were delighted to see her. They were perfectly willing to chat. One filed a complaint about the quality of last month's titles, while the other told her how good they'd been. But neither knew anything about Valerie St John.

'Tell her we'd love to have an autograph party,' one of them called after Shelby as she left. 'It would pull people in from all over the state!'

Shelby shuddered. If Valerie heard a whisper of that, she'd never come out of hiding.

She shifted the manuscript folder to a more comfortable position and stopped at the hotel desk to buy a copy of the newspaper. It might as well go in her scrapbook, she had decided. It would probably be the only time she made the front page of any newspaper.

As she turned towards the stairs, reading the article, the woman at the desk said, 'Do you want your mail now?'

'Mail?' A postcard from Lora, perhaps? 'Sure.' A thump on the counter made her jump, and she looked up in surprise. No postcard had ever weighed that much.

On the desk was a stack of manila envelopes a foot and a half high. 'They were dropped off this afternoon,' the hotel manager said.

'All at once?'

'No. The president of the bridge club came in first with hers. Then a housewife from the east end of town. Then——'

'I get the picture,' Shelby groaned. 'Has everybody in this town written a book?'

'Not quite,' the manager said, with a smile. 'I haven't started yet. I'm still working on my outline.'

Shelby didn't stick around to listen to any more. She carried the manuscripts upstairs and dumped them on her bed. Then she leaned against the door and thought about bursting into tears. 'Valerie,' she said to the empty room, 'this is all your fault. When I get my hands on you——!'

CHAPTER FIVE

'CHRIS SINCLAIR——' Shelby muttered. She wrote it down on a slip of paper and added the title of a book on scuba diving below it. 'I've seen that name somewhere else here——'

She delved through the scraps of paper that littered the big bed, and came up with one. 'Chris Sinclair also checked out a book called *The Artistry of French Food*,' she said triumphantly, and put the two of them together. The combination definitely made Ms Sinclair a possible Valerie. The problem was, there were a half dozen others who fit the same category. All had checked out books on at least two of the four subjects Shelby and Mark had searched out at the library. But no one had, apparently, been interested in all of them.

'If Chris Sinclair is Valerie, then she must have her own books on primitive African art and premature babies. She has to have got the facts somewhere,' Shelby muttered. She wished that Mark were around. He probably knew Chris Sinclair, and all of the others whose names she had written and rewritten so patiently. Without Mark's help, all Shelby could do was look each name up in the telephone book, call the number, and ask for Valerie. 'Chancy,' she told herself. 'Very chancy.' And very easy for Valerie to deny, because Shelby's evidence was so transparently thin that not even Shelby herself was convinced.

She glanced at her watch. Past six o'clock, and she'd heard nothing from Mark since she'd walked off without a word, leaving him painting the house, that morning. Shelby supposed that it was to be expected. Why should he come looking for her? She hadn't been

especially nice to the man, and it didn't matter to him
whether she ever found Valerie or not. He had only
been helping out because Lora had asked him to do her
a favour . . .

'And there's no reason why that should make you
feel sad, dammit,' Shelby told herself crossly. 'He's an
egotistical, domineering, bossy, arrogant male, and you
don't need another one for your collection.'

Nevertheless, she decided, and reached out to stroke
the yellow silk daffodil on the night table, she ought to
at least phone him and apologise . . .

His answering machine clicked on after four rings,
and said politely, in a dulcet feminine voice, 'Mark is
busy retyping his new novel. He hates the job anyway,
and interruptions only tempt him to quit entirely. So
please tell me, at the sound of the beep, in twenty-five
words or less, why you need to talk to him. The most
original reason will win a return phone call.'

Trust Mark to own a smart-mouthed machine,
Shelby thought tartly. If he's really typing, she added to
herself, I'll eat the whole book. He's probably
entertaining the little lady who made the tape . . .

And why should that make her jealous? 'He kissed
me all of once,' she told herself sharply, 'and that one
could have taken place on the front steps of the public
library without embarrassing anyone.' Even the librarian—prude though she was—couldn't have been
offended by that kiss, Shelby was forced to admit.

She recited a taut apology that made no effort to be
cute and put the phone down, feeling as if she'd cut
herself off from something important. Which was
utterly ridiculous, she told herself, and went back to
work on her list of names.

It was lonely work, and she was beginning to feel that
the whole cause was hopeless. If Valerie didn't want to
be found, how on earth was one woman, a stranger in
town and with less than a week to look, going to break

through a cloud of anonymity that had held up for years among people the woman knew?

Right now I need a friend, Shelby told herself. She picked up the telephone and dialled Lora's apartment.

Astonishingly enough, Lora herself answered. 'Hello, darling,' she cooed. 'How is life out on the frontier? Have you been scalped yet?'

'No—but your precious Mark has threatened a couple of times.'

'How are you getting along with him?'

'We're not.'

'That's a pity.' Lora didn't sound in the least upset. 'He's a really marvellous man. A bit of a lady-killer, perhaps——'

'I'd noticed.' It would have been thoughtful of you to warn me, she almost said, but bit her tongue.

'And the elusive Valerie?'

'No traces yet. What's the news in New York?'

'I'm not sure you want to know, dear.'

Shelby groaned. 'What now?'

'Rodney was here last night. He must have a source inside Jonas Brothers.'

'He doesn't know where I am, does he? He can't—only you know.' There was accusation in Shelby's voice.

'He didn't find out from me. But he's no fool, darling, he definitely knows that you aren't spending your vacation in New England. But I don't think that's what is bothering him.'

'Oh? So what is it?'

'I'm not sure. But he dropped Maria Martin's name last night as if he'd been talking to her.'

For a split second Shelby was back in the Old Man's office, listening as he said, 'If you lose Maria Martin or Valerie St John, you're done . . .'

'Not Maria!' she wailed. 'She can't do that to me!'

'Darling, it may be nothing. Maria isn't hiding out as Valerie is—everybody knows where to find her. Rodney has certainly talked to her before, and she told him to go sit on a tack, like the sensible girl she is. But——'

'Money talks,' Shelby said bitterly.

'I shouldn't have told you,' Lora said.

'I'm glad you did. I can't find a trace of Valerie, and if Maria goes over to the enemy, I might just as well pack my bags and come on home. There's no sense in spending any more of the money I haven't got in a hopeless search.'

Lora sounded horrified. 'But it isn't certain that Maria will do anything. Shelby, if you need money I'll send you whatever you want. You mustn't give up now.'

Shelby sighed. 'Oh, I won't quit, Lora. I'm too stubborn to do that.'

'If you need anything, call me.'

'Just a ride home from the airport next weekend. Unless I find Valerie, I won't be able to afford a cab.'

She put the phone down, wishing desperately that she hadn't called Lora after all. Maria! If Maria deserted her——

There was nothing Shelby could do about it, she reflected. She certainly could do nothing more tonight. And she turned her attention back with nervous fury to the search for Valerie.

She was sitting cross-legged on her bed, surrounded by scraps of paper, each with a person's name and the title of a book on it, when there was a knock on the door.

Another manuscript arriving to join the pile that filled the rocking chair? she wondered, and debated whether to answer it at all. But she could scarcely hide out in her room for the rest of her stay—not if she wanted to find Valerie. For all Shelby knew, this might even be Valerie herself, having heard about the search——

It was Mark. She caught her breath, astonished at the

dizzy gladness that threatened to drown her. Stupid, she told herself. She didn't even mind that it wasn't Valerie, because it was Mark instead——

What is happening to you, Shelby Stuart? she asked herself crossly. *The man was born to be charming, but did you have to let yourself become a victim?*

A draught from the hall sent her slips of paper dancing across the room. Shelby swore and started to pick them up. 'You messed up my system,' she accused.

Mark tossed his corduroy jacket across the foot of the bed and stooped to retrieve a handful of scraps. 'You amaze me,' he said. 'There actually is a reason for this confetti factory?'

Shelby stood barefoot on the braided rug in the middle of the room and thought about kicking him out. He'd been in the room less than a minute and they were already throwing darts at each other. But she knew that he would only laugh at her if she tried, and that she'd end up looking silly. Besides, her heart sang, you're glad he came back, you're glad, you're glad . . .

So she gathered up the last scraps, climbed back on to the high bed, and settled herself with her back against the tall headboard to sort them out all over again.

He lounged across the foot of the bed. 'What are you doing?' he asked polite. 'If you're organising a new trivia game——'

'I'm co-ordinating the readers of all the books that we looked up at the library,' she said absently, nibbling on a fingernail.

'And have you found Valerie St Joan of Arc?'

'Not yet. No one person has checked out books in all those areas. I think we need another session.'

Mark groaned. 'I don't know why I keep coming back for more of this.'

Shelby wasn't listening. 'I have three names and a number, and I'm sure that one of them is Valerie. Probably the number, knowing Valerie,' she finished suddenly glum.

'Cheer up. Aunt Pat can find out whose number it is.'

'Sure. Next week—after it's too late to help me.'

He shrugged. 'We'll work it out. If you have to go home, Aunt Pat and I will keep looking. We're an extremely persuasive team, by the way. As soon as we find out who Miss St-George-and-the-Dragon is, Aunt Pat and I will go have a chat with her, and if Aunt Pat can't talk her into writing another book, then I'll threaten to break her legs. It works every time.'

It was silly, but Shelby felt suddenly warm and cared for. 'Do you make threats like that often?'

Mark smiled angelically. 'Just when people don't do as I like. How about dinner? I'm only a starving boy, and I haven't had a meal in at least three hours.'

Shelby raised an eyebrow. 'And I suppose if I don't want to go you'll threaten me with a broken leg?'

'Shelby!' He looked wounded. 'I'm not a violent person, most of the time. If you don't want to come with me, that's all right. I just won't tell you what I found out from Aunt Pat when she called me a few minutes ago.'

'Mark!' Her voice was hoarse with excitement. 'What did she say?'

'I'll tell you over dinner, all right? And don't dawdle. I hate to be kept hanging around.' He rolled gracefully off the bed and on to his feet. 'You have five minutes. If you're not downstairs by then I'm leaving without you.'

'Mark——'

He turned at the door with a raised eyebrow.

'Why do you keep hanging around?' It sounded ungrateful, and Shelby instantly tried to make it better. 'I mean, I'm glad you came tonight, but I treated you awfully this morning, and you can't be getting much enjoyment out of searching for Valerie——'

He smiled, and little devils danced in his eyes. Shelby held her breath. What was he going to say?

'You're down to four minutes,' he pointed out, and shut the door behind him.

She picked up one of Valerie's books from the bedside table and flung it at the door. From the other side she could hear his mocking laugh.

She had seldom dressed so fast in her life, and all the time she kept telling herself that she shouldn't bother. It was no big deal whether she went to dinner with Mark, after all. She could find out tomorrow what Patricia Buchanan had told him.

But anxiety for a new bit of information didn't explain why she was hurrying, she admitted as she pulled her favourite silk jersey dress over her head. And it didn't explain why she hadn't just combed her hair and gone with him instead of changing clothes. Her favourite dress, however, was Williamsburg blue, the precise shade that matched her eyes, and Lora had told her once it was the best colour Shelby could wear . . .

Trying to impress a man like Mark Buchanan was the stupidest thing she'd ever tried, Shelby decided. *It's a crazy infatuation*, she told herself roundly. She'd been in that position before. It should not have taken her so long to recognise the signs.

Well, Shelby told herself philosophically, at least she knew now what she was dealing with. She'd found from long experience that the best way to get over an infatuation was to go straight through it and make sure that her sense of humour didn't get bent too far out of shape in the meantime. Mark Buchanan was simply a friend of a friend, and nothing more. And after this attraction she was feeling for him had run its course, that was all he would remain—Lora's friend and client, and a pleasant memory of a week in Warren's Grove . . .

He glanced at his watch as she came down the stairs. 'You've got fifteen seconds to spare,' he told her. 'I didn't think you could do it.'

He took her to the country club again. The dining room was more crowded tonight, with nearly every table full. 'You're spending a fortune on me. At least let me buy dinner,' Shelby protested, uneasily aware that her vacation funds were already running low.

'Can't,' he said briefly, 'they don't take cash here. And only members can charge. You can do something nice for me some day.'

The sparkle in his eyes made her wonder a little uneasily what that 'something nice' might be. Then she caught her breath. For surely 'some day' implied that he was planning to see her again after this week was over . . .

And that's about enough nonsense from you, Shelby, she lectured herself. She ought to know herself better. These infatuations of hers came regularly but lasted a couple of months at most. This one, because it was more intense, would probably burn itself out much faster. By the end of the week she'd be delighted that she wouldn't see him again, Shelby told herself.

She handed the menu back to the waitress with her order and said, 'Tell me what Aunt Pat said. Sorry— you've got me into the habit of calling her that.'

'She wouldn't mind, as long as you don't call her Patty. She said that she doesn't remember any writers being employed at the library—if any librarian scribbled in her spare time, she kept it under wraps.'

Shelby's face fell. 'I thought you had some good news.'

'I'm not finished yet,' he scolded, 'be patient. Aunt Pat also racked her brain for anyone who left a library job and became mysteriously independent—started living without visible means of support, that's how she put it. No luck so far, but she'll keep thinking.'

'My patience is wearing out, Mark,' Shelby warned.

'The good news is coming. She rattled off a list of half-a-dozen heavy readers of that kind of book——'

'Mark, for heaven's sake, don't be naive. For every writer there are thousands of readers——'

He waved her to silence and continued, 'Who have publicly stated that they could write something just as good.'

Shelby shut her eyes in pain. 'Do you know how many women say that?'

He leaned back in his chair and smiled. 'Yes, but at least one of them is on your list of names—I'll bet on it. And between the two methods, I'll bet we've got Valerie St Mary of the Springs.'

Shelby was unconvinced. 'I'm putting my money on Chris Sinclair.'

'Chris Sin——' He started to chuckle, and swallowed it. 'You've got me, Shelby. Why?'

'Because she reads cookbooks and scuba manuals. Besides, if you think about it, Mark, it becomes obvious. Sinclair is just a shortened version of St Clair—it was probably changed when the family immigrated a hundred years ago. Your friend at the newspaper said that this town is family-tree crazy, remember? And from St Clair to St John requires no great burst of imagination—why are you laughing?'

He was leaning back in his chair, helpless. Finally he sat up and said, 'Because Chris Sinclair is the biggest, burliest deputy sheriff this county has ever seen.'

'A man?' Shelby asked weakly.

Mark nodded solemnly. 'He's also the official scuba rescue squad whenever someone tips a boat over in the river.'

'Oh.' Then Shelby recovered herself a bit. 'So explain the cookbooks,' she challenged.

'His wife—whose name is Ethel, by the way—runs a catering service.'

He was kind enough to give Shelby a few minutes to recover herself. Then he said, 'But your suspicions may not have been an entirely lost cause. Chris teaches scuba classes, which may have been where Valerie St James Square got the idea. I'll call him tomorrow and see if he remembers any students who took a lot of notes.'

Shelby wished that she had thought of that. She hated having to depend on Mark so much.

'Careful now,' he said, 'but look over your left shoulder. The elderly lady with the unlikely blue hair, at the table full of women.'

Shelby looked, carefully. 'So?'

'That's Aunt Pat's favourite candidate. Her name is Violet Scott. In case you didn't notice, she and Valerie St-Lawrence-Seaway share a set of initials.'

Shelby sneaked another look. *Oh, please*, she thought silently, *don't let that be Valerie. I can't bear it if she's old, and lined, and wears three strands of beads and a rhinestone ring on each finger. Not Valerie—she's young and lovely!*

For the first time, Shelby began to fear that she would find Valerie and be disappointed by the truth. Was this why Valerie had hidden behind a pen name, because the reality could not match the image of a writer of love stories?

But perhaps, Shelby thought, a little saddened at her own prejudiced reaction, young at heart is the only kind of youth that really matters. It was the inside Valerie who had written the touching books and the charming letters. That was the Valerie whom Shelby had grown to care for.

'Mrs Scott was on my list,' she recalled. 'She checked out cookbooks and a book on premature babies.' Shelby turned casually in her chair to get as good a look at the woman as possible. 'Well—it can't have been her own pregnancy she's been researching. That's one point in Aunt Pat's favour, much as I hate to admit it.'

Violet Scott saw them, and bent over the table to

speak to her companions. Then, suddenly, she beckoned imperiously to Mark.

'We've been summoned,' he muttered. 'Are you ready for this?'

'What the heck! We have to go to the salad bar in a minute anyway,' Shelby said. She didn't even notice whether she was making sense; she was too nervous to care. If Violet Scott was Valerie, this was the end of her search. And if she wasn't—would Mrs Scott simply demand to know why Shelby had been staring at her?

The three other ladies at the table were much the same age. One of them was fluttering her hands nervously; one looked bored; one was excited. Only Violet Scott was apparently calm.

'Oh, Miss Stuart,' the excited one bubbled as they neared the table, 'it's such a breathtaking experience to have you here in Warren's Grove! Why, I don't think we've ever had such a celebrity here before——'

The bored one interrupted her. 'Nonsense, Madge. Mr Buchanan is every bit as much a celebrity.'

'I'm one up on you,' Mark muttered into Shelby's ear.

'Why, Sally Evans,' the excited one answered, 'Mr Buchanan doesn't count, he's a home-town boy.'

Shelby gave Mark a twisted smile as the barb evened the score.

Mrs Evans ignored the argument and looked up at Shelby with a cold smile. 'So you're an editor? That's—very interesting.' She dismissed the subject with a wave. 'When will Patricia be back in town, Mr Buchanan?'

'Is she away?' The nervous one spoke for the first time. 'She'll miss our writers' club meeting tomorrow, then. What a shame.'

'Writers' club?' Shelby said. 'There's a writers' club in Warren's Grove?' Beside her, Mark made a sound that might have been a warning, but she ignored him. In for a penny, in for a pound, she thought. Besides, she must already have every manuscript in town in her possession—what harm could it do to go to a club meeting?

'Why, we should have you come and speak to us, Miss Stuart,' the nervous woman said. 'Of course! Why didn't I think of that before?'

'Because her photograph was only in the paper this morning,' the bored one pointed out coolly.

'I'm really not a speaker,' Shelby said quickly, 'but I'd like to come to the meeting, if I may.'

Violet Scott had not said a word. Now she spoke ponderously, in a surprisingly deep voice. 'I hardly think it's appropriate to invite Miss Stuart without the consent of the club, Nora. Membership is by invitation only, you know.'

'Of course I know.' Nora—the nervous one—bridled. 'I helped you found the club, Violet. I certainly know the rules. The meeting tomorrow is at my house, and I'm issuing the invitation. So there!'

'Oh, I think everyone will be so thrilled,' the excited woman fluttered. 'I'm sure it will be just fine with everyone, Violet.' She turned to Shelby. 'Miss Stuart, do you think, if I brought my copies of Valerie St John's books with me tomorrow, that you could get her to autograph them?'

Shelby swallowed hard, but before she could find her voice, the bored woman had intervened. 'Gladys, don't be ridiculous. Of course she can't; she can't find this woman—whatever her name is—at all. Mr Buchanan, please tell Patricia that I have the arrangements made for that family-tree workshop she's to give at the historical society at the end of the month. Ask her to call me when she returns home, please.'

'I'll bet I know who it is,' Nora said suddenly. 'I was in the library the other day, and——'

Everything led back to the library, Shelby thought, and held her breath. Was Nora the one person in Warren's Grove who knew?

'Nora!' Violet Scott boomed. 'This is mere idle speculation.'

'That's right, Nora,' the bored woman agreed. 'It doesn't look good at all for you to be gossiping like this.'

Nora subsided.

Shelby stifled a sigh. Well, she could at least talk to her tomorrow. 'Where will the writers' club meet?' she asked.

'My house is three doors up the hill from Pat's,' Nora said. 'Mr Buchanan knows. Two o'clock.'

I'll be there fifteen minutes early if it kills me, Shelby thought. *And I hope they haven't convinced you by then to keep quiet* ... She looked up at Mark, and disappointment must have glowed in her eyes.

She was almost in tears by the time they were back at their table. 'So close,' she said, 'and so damned far away, all at the same time.'

'It looks as if Aunt Pat may have been right,' Mark observed. 'Violet Scott was certainly nervous, wasn't she?'

'If she's Valerie, I'll sit down and cry,' Shelby announced.

'So much for friendship?' But Mark's tone was understanding. 'Valerie St Bernard would have been a better choice of name for her.'

Shelby giggled as she blotted a suspicious dab of moisture from her eyelashes. 'Violet is a real dog,' she agreed. 'So your Aunt Pat belongs to the writers' club?'

Mark nodded. 'So do half of the women in town. It's just another excuse for them to get together and gossip.'

'I see. And you? Are you a member of the writers' club?'

He choked on his wine. 'You must be joking! I didn't get five spy thrillers written by reading selections to a bunch of tabbies over a tea-table, Shelby.'

Shelby shrugged. 'I'd think that as a writer——'

'No, Shelby. The members of that club don't write—they just sit around and pretend that they do. Real writers don't belong to clubs. And I'm not going to the meeting tomorrow, either. I'll point you in the right direction, but then you're on your own.'

'Some assistant you are,' she sniffed.

He merely smiled, and Shelby's heart did a flip. 'It won't work, dear heart,' he said. 'All four of them are on Aunt Pat's list, by the way.'

'Of possible suspects? You're joking. I'd bet that the one who kept making the catty remarks—what was her name?'

'Sally Evans.'

'I'll bet she's never read a romance in her life. Too trashy.'

'So much for your instincts,' Mark jeered. 'Aunt Pat says she checks them out by the truckload. Watch yourself, Shelby, and remember—when you start quizzing Nora about what she saw at the library—that you might be talking to Valerie St Ives herself.'

CHAPTER SIX

'I'M beginning to think I need a scorecard to keep track of all the suspects!' Shelby wailed. 'I must be up to an even dozen by now, and they all look equally likely——'

'Except for Chris Sinclair,' Mark said. He was trying not to smile.

Shelby glared at him. 'Maybe it's his wife,' she said firmly.

Mark cut thoughtfully into his steak. There was a long silence, and then he said, 'I know where she is! We've all slipped up. Valerie St Petersburg is really Agnes.'

Shelby shook her head, trying to get her thoughts to settle down into some sort of pattern. 'Now you have me honestly confused. Do we even have an Agnes?'

'Oh, yes. The woman at the newspaper office who knows all and tells all—remember?'

Shelby groaned. 'How could I have forgotten her name—and her bridge club? Why do you think that she could be——?'

'It's obvious,' he said, as if he were instructing a kindergartener. 'She is spreading fact and rumour indiscriminately around town—right?'

'Right.'

'And the result is——'

'A whole roomful of manuscripts,' Shelby sighed, remembering the rocker loaded down with manila envelopes.

'That's right. And you're kept so busy coping with frustrated authors and reading manuscripts that you have no time to spare for thinking about Agnes.'

'I think a lot about Agnes, mainly nasty thoughts every time I look around my room. I'm astonished, with the publicity that she's given me, that no one has yet followed me into the ladies' room somewhere——'

'That's exactly what I mean. You certainly aren't suspecting that she's Valerie Mount St Helens in disguise.'

Shelby frowned thoughtfully while she ate an entire plate of shrimp. Mark demolished his steak and said, 'As long as you're being quiet—I have some more ideas for our new book.'

Shelby groaned. 'Not the house painter again.'

He nodded cheerfully. 'This is a winner, Shelby. The plot just keeps flowing smoothly along. Our hero can be a real drip sometimes, and the heroine is a little flaky, but they keep patching the relationship up——'

'I wish you'd go back to spy stories,' she said tartly.

Mark, feigning hurt feelings, fell silent.

Finally Shelby said, 'This whole thing with Valerie is giving me a headache.'

'I shouldn't wonder. Shall I ask the waitress to put aspirin sauce on your ice cream sundae?'

Shelby ignored him. 'Have you finished reading Valerie's book yet?'

'No. Happy endings have no suspense, so I quit halfway through. Halfway through Chapter One, that is.'

'I keep thinking that if you would read them with an open mind, you might see something that I'm missing.' Shelby's voice was pleading.

Mark's eyebrows shot up. 'Do I hear a trace of humility in that voice? From an editor? Will wonders never cease?'

How did she ever convince herself she was attracted to this arrogant brute? Shelby wondered irritably. As an infatuation, this one might get the world's record for brevity. 'Only because you know this town better than I do,' she snapped. 'Valerie writes a lot about a fictional small town, and obviously the small town is Warren's Grove.'

'What's obvious about that?'

'Why should she make up things when she has a whole town right in front of her? And if there ever was a town populated by characters——'

'I get the point, Shelby. You can come down off the soapbox now. What do you want me to do?'

'Read the books,' she begged, reaching across the table to put her hand confidingly in his. 'See if you can recognise things that exist in Warren's Grove. If something was important enough to her to put it into a book, then——'

He picked up the idea. 'Then we can use it as an elimination test on our suspects. Frankly, I can't see walking up to Violet Scott and asking if she's ever been inside the Sand Bar, but——'

'Will you do it? Read the books, I mean, not interrogate Mrs Scott.'

Mark sighed. 'Are you giving me a choice?' He scrawled his name across the bottom of the bill and held her chair. 'I'm sure you have a full set of Valerie St Augustine's masterpieces at the hotel.'

Shelby gave him her warmest smile. 'I promise you won't regret it, Mark. It might even open up a whole new world for you.'

He grunted. 'Now *I* have a headache.'

She broke the silence in the car. 'Did you ask the librarian about Valerie's autograph in that book you checked out?'

He nodded. 'She seemed to think you'd done it to kick off your publicity campaign.'

Shelby's jaw dropped. 'She thought I'd——'

'Come to think of it ...' Mark looked her over-curiously in the glare of a street light. 'Did you?'

'Mark! Why would I sign Valerie's name on a book?'

He shrugged. 'Why not? You're the one who says it's authentic, and you're the only expert we have when it comes to Valerie's handwriting.'

Shelby was stunned. 'I didn't have the chance. I never touched that book——'

'I suppose you could have a secret knack for picking pockets. Or maybe——' he snapped his fingers. 'I've got it! There is no Valerie St-Valentine's-Day-Massacre at all. You made the whole thing up just to get close to me.'

Shelby clenched her fists. This has been the shortest infatuation in history, she reminded herself. 'Why on earth would I do that?' she asked baldly. 'Who would go to this much touble just to meet you?'

'Aunt Pat says I'm charming.'

'Your Aunt Pat is prejudiced! Where are we going?'

'Aspirin,' he said briefly, parking the car in front of the all-night drugstore. 'I have a feeling we're both going to need it before the evening is over.'

She checked the book section. Valerie's latest romance had sold out, but her own face stared at her from the newspaper clipping taped to the rack. The manager of the book department wasn't going to miss out on the free publicity! She ruffled through the other books and picked up a paperback copy of one of Mark's spy thrillers.

'You have enough to read without wasting your time on that,' he recommended over her shoulder. 'Shelby, look who I ran into. This is Chris Sinclair.'

Mark was tall, but the man standing beside him made him look like a pigmy. The deputy sheriff was built like a Sherman tank, with shoulders that would barely fit through the average doorway. He was in uniform, and his wide-brimmed hat perched atop his head like a beanie.

Shelby was still looking bemused when Mark said, 'Chris remembers having a couple of people in scuba class who spent more time asking questions than diving.'

'If Violet Scott was one of them, I'll send your Aunt Pat a dozen roses,' Shelby muttered.

'No, but one of them was the girl who brought her manuscript up to the house this morning.'

'She said she wanted to get into shape,' the deputy rumbled. His voice was so deep that it seemed to start at his toes. 'Didn't look like she needed it, though. She tosses those books around all day—I should think that would be exercise enough.'

'She tosses—what books?' Shelby asked.

'She's the one who puts all the books back on the shelves at the library,' he said. 'You know, after they've returned and checked back in——'

Shelby turned on Mark. 'You didn't tell me that!'

'I didn't know it,' he protested. 'Why do you think I'm supposed to know everything?'

'Because you seem to think you do,' she snapped. 'Thank you, Mr Sinclair. You've been very helpful indeed!' She put Mark's book back on the shelf and grabbed his arm. 'Come on, let's get back to the hotel. I told you that Valerie had something to do with the library!'

'If I might ask just one small, stupid question . . .' Mark said, as she dragged him out to the car.

'What about it?' Shelby asked impatiently.

'If she's Valerie, why did she beg you to read her manuscript? Why didn't she just tell you who she is?'

'Because she didn't want me to know——' Shelby's voice trailed off.

'In that case,' Mark asked reasonably, 'why didn't she stay home and hide the envelope on the top shelf of her linen closet? Why force you to notice her if she didn't want to be found out? It's a contradiction in terms.'

Shelby was silent for a long moment. 'I still want to read that manuscript of hers right away.'

'Anything you say, sweetheart. But can I pick up Aunt Pat's mail first? I forgot it this afternoon, and she's expecting an important letter.'

'Sure.' Shelby was distracted, but when he got out of the car in front of the post office she scrambled out too. Would her note to Valerie still be there, or had the woman picked up her mail on the sly sometime in the last two days?

But the envelope was still there. 'I don't know whether to be happy or sad,' Shelby said. 'It might mean that she's out of town and doesn't know anything about the fuss. Or it could mean that she knows all about it and simply doesn't want to have anything to do with me. And I don't even know which would be worse!'

'Or possibly,' Mark said as he flipped through Aunt Pat's mail, 'she's locked herself in her room and is producing the world's greatest romance novel—goodness, talk about a contradiction!—so she can surprise you with it. Ah. Here's Aunt Pat's important letter. I'd better go home and call her. I'll pick up the books tomorrow.'

'Hold it!' Shelby commanded. 'Why don't you use my phone, and start reading the books tonight?'

Mark grinned and snapped his fingers. 'Foiled again.'

The sparkle in his eyes made Shelby's heart melt all over again. She ought to know better, she thought. But the man was so darned charming when he tried . . .

There was another pile of manuscripts at the hotel desk. The manager handed them to Shelby with an apologetic glance. 'I told them you were too busy to read all these things,' she said, 'but they just dumped them off anyway. I'm sorry, Miss Stuart.'

'It certainly isn't your fault,' Shelby told her, eyeing the pile with distaste. 'I'm sorry to be such a bother.'

'Oh, and you had a phone call earlier. It was a correspondent for a daily newspaper up in the state capital. They read the story in the paper here and wanted to talk to you.'

Shelby groaned. 'That's all I need. Are they going to call back?'

'Tomorrow some time. Is Mr Buchanan going to help read some of those manuscripts tonight?' At Shelby's nod, the manager said, 'I'll bring up a pot of hot chocolate for you when I go off duty. You'll need it, and the coffee shop will be closed by then.'

'She certainly takes good care of you,' Mark commented. He took the pile of evelopes out of Shelby's arms so that she could unlock her door.

'I know, it's like living at home all over again. Except my mother would have reminded me to leave my door open if I insisted on taking you up to my room.'

'Oh. In that case, I'm glad she isn't your mother.' He dropped the manuscripts on the braided rug and tossed himself down on the bed. 'Take me, I'm yours,' he murmured, his eyes closed.

For an instant, seeing that long, lean body sprawled on her bed, Shelby was tempted to forget about work and take him up on the offer. What would it be like to sleep with Mark Buchanan? she wondered, and suffered a pang of jealousy as she realized that Lora, without a doubt, knew exactly how it felt.

Then she resolutely pushed temptation behind her and dropped Valerie's first book on to his chest. 'Don't try to distract me,' she warned.

He jumped as if he'd been hit by a bullet, and said reproachfully, 'I was just providing the appropriate atmosphere. If you're going to be reading romance, after all——'

'Call Aunt Pat and then get down to work,' she ordered.

She retreated to the bathroom to change into a fleecy jogging suit so that she could be comfortable, and when she returned, Mark's jacket and tie were draped over the foot of the bed and he was stretched out under the handmade quilt, talking on the phone.

Shelby stopped dead in the doorway, shakily wondering what he'd done with the rest of his clothes. Then he stretched, and she realized that he was fully dressed except for his shoes. With a totally irrational feeling of regret, she crossed the room with a pile of manuscripts and curled up at the head of the bed.

'Do you want to know what she's like, Aunt Pat?' Mark said into the phone, with a sideways grin at Shelby. 'She's my kind of girl. We do our best research in bed.'

If it hadn't been for the gleam in his eyes, Shelby would have hit him right then. But that, she thought regretfully, would only give him an opportunity to back out of working, and she needed his help tonight. So she studiously avoided his eyes and opened the first manuscript—the one the girl had pushed into her arms in front of Patricia Buchanan's house. Had it only been that morning? she wondered. It felt like for ever ago.

Mark cupped a hand over the phone. 'What's that library card number you were trying to track down? Aunt Pat says she's served so many volunteer hours there that she might have it memorised.'

Shelby scrambled her slips of paper, and pulled the number out. Mark read it into the phone. There was a long silence, and then he whooped with laughter. 'Now that is what I call conscientious,' he said. 'Patty, you're a jewel.'

'I thought she didn't like being called Patty,' Shelby muttered.

'Any other ideas?' Mark asked his aunt. 'All right. See you Monday. The housepainting will be done if I don't go too far afield hunting for Valerie St Christopher's Medal.' He put the phone down and lay back against Shelby's pillow, laughing.

'Who did my suspect turn out to be?'

He sat up and wiped tears from his eyes. 'That card number is registered to the head librarian herself. Miss Branch is so careful with the public's property that she even checks out her own books—and, no doubt, pays the fines if she forgets to return them on time! So much for your methods, Shelby.'

'She hardly seems the type to nurture a passion for African art,' Shelby muttered.

'Oh, I don't know. She probably took it home when it was brand new so she could recommend it to the patrons.' He picked up the paperback and squinted at it. 'Must I?' he asked, his eyes wide and pleading as he turned to her.

'You must.' Shelby reached for her glasses in the night-table drawer.

'Hey, you look good in those,' Mark said.

Shelby shrugged. 'I only wear them when I have to do a lot of reading. I read five thousand manuscripts a year, and the pace has ruined my eyes.'

Mark shuddered. 'I suppose I should count my blessings that I only have to read—how many books?'

'Valerie has written six altogether. Three of them are small-town settings, so if you read all of those——'

'Will I have earned your undying gratitude?' He turned his back to her and opened the book.

Silence fell, broken only by the rustle of paper as Shelby paged through the first manuscript. 'Much as I hate to admit it,' she said a few minutes later as she put it aside, 'you're right. Our book-shelver is no Valerie, that's sure. No power, no depth—not even any originality.'

Mark mumbled something. He didn't even look at her.

She suspected darkly that he was dozing, but she didn't want to start another argument, so she picked up the next envelope.

It was an hour later when Mark moved. He'd turned

a page now and then, but Shelby wondered if he'd really read anything at all.

'Talk about ghost-writers,' he said, 'Valerie St-Elmo's-Fire is the worst.'

'What is that supposed to mean?'

He tossed the book aside. 'This whole thing happened here. Ten years ago or so. She fictionalised the incident, imagined the characters past all logic, made up her own conclusion, and called it a book.'

'You're joking!' Shelby grabbed for the paperback.

'Not I.'

'But how do you know?'

He raised an eyebrow. 'Didn't you recognise me? I'm the tall, dark mysterious stranger who, no doubt, does not get the girl on the last page.'

'Poor Mark,' Shelby mourned. 'What a bruise for your ego!'

'It's well done,' he admitted. 'If I hadn't been told flat out that Valerie St Malo was writing about Warren's Grove, I might not have remembered that old incident. It is ancient history, after all. But——'

'Do you suppose that's why she's hiding out?'

'Go to the head of the class,' he mocked. 'There are people in this town who would be tempted to sue her over that book, Shelby.'

'But if it's been fictionalised——'

'I didn't say they could collect,' he reminded. 'But they might set out to make her life a little unpleasant. No, I think she's being very wise to stay under wraps.'

'But that means I may never find her!'

'You could put an ad in the personal column,' Mark suggested. 'Promise to keep her secret if she'll just call you.'

'Mark, be serious.'

'I always am. You may not want to find Valerie St Vitus Dance after all, Shelby. Jonas Brothers might not be too pleased to find themselves in court, and I don't imagine your boss would look kindly on you for making it happen ... Give me that book back. I want to find out if I should call my lawyer in the morning.'

Shelby tried to read another manuscript, but her mind was running around in circles. She was trying desperately to remember the details of Valerie's first book. Was it possible that Mark was right?

He had turned to the last chapter, and when he had finished, he put the book down with a sigh.

'Well?' Shelby asked eagerly. 'Are you going to sue her?'

'What?' He looked horrified. 'Sue a genius like that, a writer with such an uncanny perception of character?'

'Oh, now I understand. She let you get the girl after all.'

'No. But I didn't want her, so that's all right.'

'Mark, you're hopeless! Would you be serious for two minutes?'

'If I must. I think Valerie St-Louis-Blues pulled it off, Shelby.'

'So she can come out of hiding without worrying.' Shelby's face was aglow.

'But she may not realize that,' Mark warned. He picked up the second book. 'As for the town itself—I don't see much of Warren's Grove in here. Have you ever considered that Valerie may live somewhere else, and just come into Warren's Grove now and then to pick up her mail?'

Shelby thought about it. 'It makes sense,' she said reluctantly. 'Sometimes it's weeks after I write before I hear from her.'

'Just a thought,' Mark murmured, and opened the book.

Shelby went back to reading manuscripts. Most of them she dismissed after ten minutes of skim-reading; for many of them, it took her longer to write a brief, thoughtful note to the author than it had to diagnose the manuscript as impossible.

She wished that she'd brought a supply of printed rejection slips along. Her hand was beginning to cramp.

'You know, it really infuriates me when people think that just anyone can write a romance novel,' she said.

'Hmmm.' Mark didn't take his eyes off the page.

'They think that if they string together twelve chapters of clichés that they'll have a sure-fire seller— Mark?'

'Were you talking to me?' He looked up finally.

'Are you ready to join Valerie's fan club or what? I didn't expect you to read every word, just the sections that describe the little town.'

'It's fascinating to see which cliché she'll use next.' he said.

'You weren't even listening to me!' Shelby accused.

He'd turned back to the book. 'Well, no, I wasn't,' he admitted. 'I've finally reached the love scene, and I'd hate to miss any of it.'

'Don't let me interrupt your enjoyment,' Shelby snapped, and reached for another manuscript.

Mark didn't even answer, but five minutes later he started to laugh.

'The love scene is not supposed to be funny,' Shelby informed him loftily.

'Who checks the facts in these things?' he demanded. 'All these heroes must be Olympic class weightlifters, the way they carry the girls around——'

'A ninety-eight pound weakling isn't particularly romantic to think about,' Shelby pointed out.

'And then there's this thing——' He shook the paperback under her nose. 'The guy's a certified flying instructor, for heaven's sake!'

'So? Is it a felony or something?'

'Any teacher worth his salt has better sense than to try to seduce his student in the front seat of a single-engine airplane during a lesson.'

'He's terribly in love with her,' Selby pointed out.

'And he's going to be terribly dead if he keeps it up! That plane isn't going to stay in the air just because he tells it to. Somebody has to pay some attention. Shelby, have you ever flown in a small plane? I mean, a really small plane?'

'No. I was going to take the commuter flight out here, but——'

'Wise choice. I suspect that it's sometimes late because they make a crop-dusting detour. Well, Valerie is obviously not a flyer either, or she'd have known that there just isn't enough room for this kind of hijinks in a trainer plane.'

'There isn't?'

'Worse than a sports car,' he said briefly. 'And speaking of sports cars——' He tapped the cover of the first book he'd thrown aside. 'Undressing the heroine in the front seat of the Maserati would have been difficult enough. Getting her clothes back on would be impossible. Valerie certainly goes in for kinky seduction scenes, doesn't she?'

'I'll bet the ones in your books aren't exactly family-orientated,' Shelby argued.

'True. Two points for you.' He picked up the third book. 'What happens in this one? Does our hero demonstrate his undying passion on the back of a horse? Or in a canoe while they're shooting rapids? Or perhaps——'

'Mark, just shut up and read the book. I didn't ask you to play literary critic.'

'I wonder how she tests these ideas out,' he mused. 'Or perhaps she just leaves it to you—basic fact-checking is the editor's job, after all.' He was leafing through the book. 'Dreadful to have to wade through all this other stuff to find the five pages of love scenes ... Here's the first one.' He scanned it rapidly. 'Valerie St. Veronica's Veil, you disappoint me. An ordinary bedroom.'

'Doesn't anything please you, Mark?'

He was absorbed in the page. '"He carried her across the room and flung her on the bed, and was beside her before she could roll away from him." What a fairytale! If any ordinary man tried this, he'd get slapped. Let me demonstrate.'

'Give me that book,' Shelby argued.

Mark put it in her hand. 'Since you're already on the bed, I won't argue about the preliminaries. Any ordinary man would have thrown his back out carrying you across the room and would be unable to do anything about it now that you're in bed, but we won't argue that one.'

'I'm not that heavy!' Shelby argued.

'Not you specifically. I was referring to the generic heroine. I know she never weighs more than a hundred and two, but that's still like tossing around a bale of cotton. All right—he's grabbed her against her will, carried her across the room, and dumped her into his bed. What comes next?'

Shelby gave him a jaundiced look and glanced at the page. 'His lips scorched the silken skin of her inner arm——'

'Ah, yes. And what is she doing with the other hand right now, I ask you? Unless this girl is a moron, she's probably pulling his hair out. And since he hasn't put a gag in her mouth, she's also no doubt screaming bloody murder. In the meantime, what is he doing?' His voice was a little muffled by the fleecy sleeve of her jogging suit as he imitated Valerie's hero. 'He's kissing her hand like a gentleman ... I trust she wasn't wearing a long flannel nightie when he did this. If she was, he'd have got a mouthful of fuzz and probably choked to death on it——'

Shelby giggled and tugged her hand out of his grip, and Mark raised his head. 'See? You laughed at me and then pulled away. Nothing to it. But Valerie's heroine,

on the contrary, was supposed to be petrified with fear.
It was a totally unrealistic reaction to have.'

'Mark, do be serious!'

He drew back and gave her a half-smile. 'Very well,
my dear, I'll do that,' he said, softly. 'Now if the hero
had just changed his tactics a little——'

He shifted slightly on the bed, and abruptly Shelby
found herself helpless, pinned to the quilt by his weight,
her wrists caught in an iron grip. 'Let's see you get
away now,' he suggested silkily.

She struggled for a moment, and he laughed at her,
drew her hands together so he could hold both of them
with one of his, and traced the path of an ash-blonde
lock of hair with his fingertip. He gently removed her
glasses and put them safely back on the night-table.
'You wouldn't want to explain how they got broken,'
he said. Then his hand slid to the front of her jogging
suit and toyed with the zipper, pulling it down so slowly
that the release of each tooth seemed a separate click
that grated against her nerves.

A tinge of fear cooled Shelby's veins. She wasn't
afraid of him; she knew that Mark had no intention of
hurting her. But she was afraid of herself. There was a
breathless agony deep inside her, born of helplessness
and longing. She had wanted this, she thought, almost
since the first moment she had seen him, down in the
coffeeshop the morning that he had studied her as if she
were a museum display. And now that she was here in
his arms——

'I could scream,' she threatened. It was almost a
croak.

Mark smiled and shook his head. 'Before you could
open your mouth, I'd be doing this——' His lips
claimed hers in a harsh, demanding kiss that threatened
to smother her.

Shelby sighed, a little animal moan deep in her
throat, and relaxed against him, her body welcoming

the warmth and strength of his, pulling him down closer and closer, begging him with every cell to make love to her.

I've never felt this way about a man before, she thought hazily. *This is the craziest infatuation I've ever fallen into . . .*

His grip on her wrists loosened, and his kisses gentled as he felt her surrender. 'Shelby——' he murmured, and his voice tickled her ear. 'See how easy it is, if Valerie's hero only knew how?'

Shelby uttered a furious little scream and tried to push him away. Mark just lay there and laughed at her, holding her without apparent effort as she struggled to escape from him.

Then, suddenly, the laughter vanished. She lay quiet in the circle of his arms and stared up into his eyes, which had turned almost black. And she thought. *This isn't an infatuation at all. I've fallen in love with him.*

CHAPTER SEVEN

OH, don't be ridiculous, Shelby told herself sharply. She'd been in love a hundred times since she was sixteen, and the average endurance was a month. As soon as the man of the moment displayed his clay feet, she fell out of love just as promptly as she'd fallen in.

She knew the stages well, and she could tell the precise moment when she went from attraction to infatuation to disillusionment to despair. But this time—well, Mark had been displaying his less-than-attractive characteristics regularly since the moment she'd met him. And it didn't seem to make any difference in how she felt.

He sensed the change in her as surely as if she had shouted it. He whispered her name, very softly, and kissed her again. The brush of his lips was like a flame across her sensitive skin as he teased her with kisses on her eyelids, her throat, the delicate lobe of her ear.

The zipper in the front of her running suit yielded to his impatient fingers, and Mark bent his head, a gleam of triumph in his dark eyes, to nibble her breast. 'Thoughtful of you not to put on a bra,' he murmured, and Shelby sighed deep in her throat, giving herself up to enjoyment.

A knock sounded at the door.

Mark froze, his hand tensing against the curve of her breast.

'The hot chocolate,' Shelby whispered.

'Would you rather drink that stuff or make love?'

'That's not the right question,' she said softly. 'I have to answer the door. Let me go, please.'

He did, reluctantly. Shelby zipped her jacket, ran a hand over her tumbled hair, and opened the door.

The hotel manager raised an eyebrow when she saw Mark sprawled across Shelby's bed, but she didn't comment. She merely handed Shelby a wooden tray that held a chubby ceramic pot and two cups and said, 'I was later than I'd expected in getting everything finished. I hope I didn't——' she coloured a little— 'interrupt anything. Good night, Miss Stuart—Mr Buchanan.'

'She knows damn' well what she interrupted,' Mark muttered as soon as the door was closed. 'Put that thing down and come back here.'

Shelby sniffed the aroma coming from the pot and shook her head. 'Thanks, but I think I'll drink my hot chocolate. Would you like some?'

'You're a tease, Shelby Stuart,' he grumbled. 'You know precisely what I'd like, and it isn't hot chocolate.'

She avoided looking at him, knowing that the invitation in his eyes would draw her right back into his arms. She was grateful for the interruption. It had given her a few moments to think about what she was doing—but now she was confused. She wasn't sure what she wanted.

I've known this man just a little more than two days, she told herself, *and ten minutes ago I was ready to make love with him. What has happened to me? I've never felt this way before.*

But a little voice in the back of her mind argued, It doesn't feel as if you just met him. It feels as if you've known him for ever. And if he's what you want, how on earth could sleeping with him be wrong?

So Shelby sipped her hot chocolate, and kept her eyes safely away from Mark, and let the argument go on inside her head.

He reached for his tie. 'If I didn't know better, I'd swear that you two planned that interruption,' he said.

'Here's Mom, right on schedule to rescue her little darling—— How do they always know, dammit?'

'Instinct,' Shelby murmured.

'She takes extraordinarily good care of you, doesn't she? It's as if she has some investment in your safety . . .'

'You needn't sound so upset. There was nothing personal about it, Mark.'

'That's right, dear heart. And there was nothing particularly personal about what she interrupted, either, was there? Just a little entertainment to wind up the evening.'

'Mark! That's not fair! I wanted——' She stopped.

Mark raised an eyebrow, and said smoothly. 'Yes, Shelby? Tell me about what you wanted.'

'I—I'm not sure.' It was a bare whisper. He was so tall, standing there at the foot of the bed, that she felt tiny and helpless.

'Well, let me know when you decide.' He knotted the tie with the swift sureness of long practice. 'She wouldn't happen to be Valerie Jolly Old St. Nicholas, would she?'

'Are you referring to the manager? You must be joking.'

Mark shrugged. 'She certainly watches out for you, as you seem to think Valerie would.'

'She couldn't be Valerie. That woman is the only person in town who isn't writing a book. She told me so herself.'

'But then,' Mark pointed out smoothly, 'Valerie isn't writing a book just now, either.' He reached for his jacket. 'See you tomorrow, dear heart.'

The door, as it closed behind him, made an oddly final click.

The telephone shrilling on the night-table brought her to full attention with a jerk. 'If that's Mark wanting me to help paint,' she muttered furiously, 'I'm going to tell him to go jump into the river. Anybody who can be cheerful at this ungodly hour of the morning——'

Her travel alarm said, however, that it was almost noon. Shelby shook her head to clear it, wondering how she could have overslept so badly. But she knew that there was really no mystery about that at all, for despite the hot chocolate it had been hours before sleep had come to her, hours when she lay wide-eyed and regretting that she had sent Mark away last night.

It all happened so suddenly, she told herself. If she'd had a chance to think about it——

And now that she'd had a chance to think, she knew that Mark had been absolutely right about one thing last night. She'd been a tease, and it would serve her right if he wanted nothing else to do with her.

Unless it was him on the phone after all——

She seized it eagerly, but it was only the stringer for the daily newspaper upstate, wanting to do a story on the exciting search for Valerie St. John. Shelby declined, as politely as possible, and put the phone down while the reporter was still arguing. Any more publicity would only drive Valerie further into hiding, Shelby thought. Besides, it was Wednesday, and by the time any new story could appear, Shelby herself would probably be on her way back to New York.

She lay there for a few minutes, propped up on the pillows, trying to gather her determination to start the day. The writers' club would meet this afternoon, and she was determined to be at Nora's house early. It was her best remaining hope of finding Valerie before the week expired.

'The whole thing is coming apart in my hands,' she said aloud. Her hopes for locating Valerie were fading, and if Lora's suspicions had been right about Maria Martin leaving Jonas Brothers——

Shelby wondered vaguely if there would be any

further news this morning about Maria. The woman was almost as popular with the readers as Valerie was, and if Maria had decided to desert Jonas Brothers for another company, Shelby might as well give up the search for Valerie entirely. No amount of explanation could save her at that point, she was certain. Bob Jonas would have her job so fast that she'd be lucky to get out of the office with her pencil-holder.

I might just as well know the bad news before I get out of bed, she thought, and called the office.

The secretary who answered said, 'Oh! Miss Stuart. I'm so glad you called,' and put her on hold before Shelby could even ask why she was so delighted.

'This does not sound promising,' she muttered, and listened to the seconds click away.

The assistant editor who had the office next to Shelby's eventually picked up the phone. 'Where have you been hiding out?' she demanded. 'We've been looking all over New England for you.'

Shelby's heart sank. 'I'm on vacation, remember?' she asked crisply. 'What's Maria Martin up to?'

'Maria?' The editor sounded intrigued. 'Nothing, as far as I know. Why?'

'Rumour has it——' Then Shelby stopped. There was no point in putting her own head in a noose; if there was nothing to Lora's rumour, why publicise it? And even if Lora was right, if Jonas Brothers didn't already know it, Shelby didn't want to be the one to tell the company. 'Never mind. Why were you looking for me?'

'Because everyone knows how you feel about Valerie's mail, and there is a letter here from her. Should I open it and read it to you?'

Shelby's hand clenched on the phone. A letter from Valerie? But that must mean——

It could mean anything, she told herself firmly. It could be that Valerie was ready to write again, but it could also be that she was upset at Shelby for trying to hunt her down and was filing a protest . . .

She sighed. Much as she wanted to know what that letter said, she didn't dare take the chance of letting its contents become public knowledge. If she were in the office she could at least do something to limit the damage. But when she was halfway across the country, anything negative in that letter would have swept the company before she could get on the train.

'Shelby?' the assistant said. 'Are you still there?'

'Don't open it,' Shelby told her, 'just leave it on my desk.'

'But shouldn't someone take care of it? I mean, if it's something urgent——'

'It can wait till Monday,' Shelby insisted.

'Whatever you say,' the assistant said. She sounded puzzled. 'Where are you, anyway? We checked with the tour group, and they said you'd cancelled——'

'I told you,' Shelby said, 'I'm on vacation. Not to be located. See you Monday.' She put the phone down. 'I should have asked what the postmark was,' she muttered. 'With my luck, Valerie is probably off lying on a beach somewhere. But if that letter was mailed in Warren's Grove . . .'

It wasn't worth another phone call to find out, and it would only arouse suspicion if she called back with such a stupid-sounding question. She kept telling herself that while she showered and put on her best suit, a cream-coloured linen that accented her upswept hair and made her look extremely professional. She hoped that it worked on the ladies at the writers' club.

Mark was painting window trim on the second floor. 'Grab a brush,' he called. 'This kind of detail is women's work, anyway.'

'I'm all dressed up.'

He turned around on the ladder. 'I'll say.' Even from

that distance, she could see warm appreciation in his eyes, and it brought a shiver to Shelby's spine.

'Are you coming along?' she asked.

'To the writers' club? What a joke.'

'I'd really like to have you come with me, Mark.'

'Too bad, dear heart. When did you call my answering service, by the way?'

'Last night. Why?'

'I know it was last night, but was it before or after we had dinner? The message you left said you were very sorry. I just wondered what you were sorry about.'

'Well, I didn't call to tell you I regretted not sleeping with you, that's sure,' Shelby snapped. 'You have the largest ego of any man west of the Great Lakes——'

'Hold it,' he commanded. 'I was simply asking a question. If you don't have enough sense to mention what time you called, you should expect questions like——'

'Nosey questions, is what I call them,' Shelby snapped. 'If you don't want to be confused by your answering service, Mark Buchanan, don't set it so it cuts off every message in thirty seconds!'

'If the all-powerful Being created the universe in six days,' Mark pointed out reasonably, 'it shouldn't take longer than half a minute to arrange a lunch date.'

'That's a typical male attitude,' Shelby sniffed. 'Who's the sweetheart on the tape, by the way? I bet all your men friends call up just to listen to her.'

He rewarded her with a grin. 'Jealous, dear heart?'

'Are you joking? I've never been jealous in my life, and certainly not of some sexy-sounding babe on an answering machine!' *Yes, I am,* she thought. *I'm dying to know who she is, and if she means anything to you . . . and where I fit into your life, if there's any room for me there at all.*

'Aunt Pat will be delighted at the compliment.'

There was a long silence, and then Shelby said, 'The

lady with the sexy voice is your Aunt Pat? I don't believe that for a minute. Would you come down off the ladder, Mark? I'm breaking my neck down here to talk to you.'

He shook his head. 'Nope. If you aren't going to help paint I have to stay with it. Someone has to do something productive here, after all.'

'Stop trying to make me feel guilty for not helping to paint your aunt's house.'

'I've spent hours and hours looking for Valerie St. Paul's Cathedral,' he pointed out reasonably.

'All right, you win. If you'll come to the meeting this afternoon, I'll help you paint tomorrow,' she said finally.

She was rewarded with a cherubic smile. 'That's my girl,' he said, and climbed down off the ladder.

And she was crazy, Shelby told herself. All he had to do was smile at her and she was lost——

He put a quick kiss on her cheek. 'I'll even let you take me to lunch,' he offered. 'How's that for generous?' He had gone into the house before she could answer.

She wandered through Patricia Buchanan's house while she waited for Mark to shower and change clothes. It reminded her of a doll's house. Pat had furnished the rooms in small-scale antiques, and the effect was of space and light and air, despite the lack of size. A bookshelf along one wall held volumes pushed in any old way. It was the only part of the room which was less than neat. Habit made Shelby glance along the row of titles. Plenty of classical literature, but no Valerie St. John. She hadn't expected any. Plants here and there softened the starkness of high ceilings and hardwood floors. Idly, Shelby checked the soil in one planter and found it bone dry.

Mark might be effective as a painter, she scolded to herself, but he had let Aunt Pat's houseplants dry up and wither away. She wandered into the kitchen, looking for a water container.

It was a big room, with a brick fireplace along one wall and dark wood cabinets on the other three sides. Pat's concessions to modern living were limited to plumbing and refrigeration; without the appliances Shelby could almost have pretended that she had walked back in time to the days when the first settlers of Warren's Grove lived here.

Then she looked closer, and was amused at her own romantic notions. She doubted that the first Warren family would have left a sack of frozen bagels on the table to thaw next to a college textbook on grammar . . .

Mark was reading up on grammar? Shelby supposed that everyone needed a refresher once in a while, but it hardly seemed typical research for him to be doing. Now if he had been studying little-known poisons and their antidotes, or the largest diamonds in the world and the mysteries and legends that surrounded them— those things would make sense.

She found a pitcher and watered Pat's plants. It took several trips to the kitchen sink, and by the time she was done Mark was downstairs. His dark hair was damp and curly, and Shelby wanted to run her fingers through it and make it all stand up on end. But she just put the pitcher up to drain and said, with a critical look at him. 'You don't look half bad when you're not covered with paint from head to foot.'

'Watch what you say,' he threatened, 'or you'll get a chance to see what it feels like to get splattered. What are you doing, anyway? Mixing martinis?' He pointed to the pitcher.

'In a manner of speaking—I was giving the plants a drink. Have you been too absorbed in grammar to remember that they're also living things and require care?

'Grammar?'

'Yes. The book.' She gave it a push. 'And you said Valerie's novels were boring!'

'That belongs to Aunt Pat. I like a little more excitement to my reading, actually. Lots of pictures, some action—you know the sort of thing.'

'Usually found in men's magazines,' Shelby said sweetly.

'That's the stuff.' He gave her a lecherous smile. 'Where are you taking me for lunch?'

As it happened, they were almost late to the writers' club meeting, and by the time they reached Nora's house her living room was full of chattering women. No men, Shelby noted.

'Why no males?' she whispered to Mark.

'See why I didn't want to come? I prefer my adoring women one at a time—I hate to be surrounded by crowds of them.' He was, within five minutes. Most of them were telling him how much they had enjoyed his new book, some wanted him to read their work and give advice.

One stout woman had attached herself to his arm like a leech and was prattling on about his Aunt Pat. Mark listened patiently and nodded, now and then trying to get a word in, but the woman didn't pause for breath. 'I enjoyed her classes so much,' she proclaimed. 'You should be proud of her——'

Mark looked a little overwhelmed, and Shelby suffered a pang of guilt for forcing him into the situation. But her regret lasted only a moment. Then she was surrounded too, and didn't have another instant to think about Mark.

She'd met with groups of writers before. This one was just as noisy, and more disorganised, than any she'd seen. Usually, though, the attention was divided; after all, wherever she went in New York, she was never the only editor present. But this—it was incredible. Every woman in the place wanted to talk to her. *Now I know*, Shelby thought, *how the settlers felt when the Indians started to circle the wagon train . . .*

It took five minutes of steady gavel-pounding before the noise died to a dull murmur and the women settled themselves into the circle of chairs in Nora's big living room.

Shelby found herself sitting next to the young woman who had brought her manuscript up to Patricia Buchanan's house the morning before. The girl looked hopeful but scared half to death, and Shelby's tender heart was touched. The manuscript was hopeless, but it had been the girl's best effort. What could she say, Shelby asked herself, that was true and yet not cruel?

'I understand you're interested in scuba diving,' she said finally.

The girl made a face. 'Not really,' she admitted, 'but I thought it might make an interesting hobby for one of my heroines. What do you think?'

'Perhaps,' Shelby tried to choose her words with care, 'but it's hard for a writer to make something interesting to a reader unless she truly cares about it.'

The girl thought that one over. 'You're saying I shouldn't write about it?'

'No, that's not what I said at all. But it may be difficult for you to make it sound good. Why not write about something you already know about?'

The girl grimaced. 'I know about ironing and changing diapers, and that's all.'

'Ladies,' said the woman with the gavel, 'the secretary will now start our meeting with the roll call of members, beginning with the charter members of our group.'

The woman who began to call off names was one of those who had been at Violet Scott's table at the country club last night, Shelby saw. She had to fumble

for the name: Madge, that was it, she finally recalled—
the one who had asked about getting Valerie to
autograph her set of books.

I'd love to oblige you, Madge, Shelby thought. *If only
I knew myself who the little lady was, I'd be happy to ask
her to sign them ... What a dumb question for the
woman to have asked.*

Or was it possible, she wondered, that Madge herself
was actually Valerie? If so, it wasn't a silly question at
all—just a bluff to throw Shelby off the track.

Mark's cynicism was beginning to take root in her,
Shelby realised as she looked around the room, noting a
familiar face here and there. He didn't believe anything
he was told, and perhaps he was right to be so
suspicious.

Any one of these women could be Valerie, she
realised. They had all given evidence of an interest in
writing, despite Mark's contention that the club was
just another social group.

Was it Violet Scott, as Patricia Buchanan thought?
The woman sat stiffly upright in her chair across the
circle, with arms folded and lips tight. She hadn't so
much as looked at Shelby, and she scarcely moved
when her name was called as a charter member. Was
this her normal attitude, Shelby wondered, or was she
upset about something?

'Patricia Buchanan is not present today,' the
secretary said, and went on with the roll.

It startled Shelby. 'Aunt Pat is a charter member?'
she muttered to Mark, who was sitting next to her,
arms folded across his chest as if he were waiting
patiently for a jury to decide his fate.

'Aunt Pat helped start everything in Warren's Grove,'
he whispered. 'Genealogy club, historical society,
Daughters of the American Revolution—She feels that
it's her responsibility as a member of the founding
family.'

'Of course,' Shelby said, 'she would.' She was almost regretting that she wouldn't be in Warren's Grove long enough to meet Patricia Buchanan; this woman must be an experience. Though, she had to admit, after what Mark had told his aunt on the phone last night Shelby wouldn't be a bit surprised if Pat rushed right home to see what he was up to.

Yet the woman couldn't be completely strait-laced, or she wouldn't put up with Mark, much less leave him alone in her house . . .

The girl next to her answered when her name was called, and the long list finally wound to an end. Shelby sighed in relief. Now they could get on to the business at hand, she thought, but she had reacted too soon.

'Now we'll have our programme,' the president announced. 'We have some very exciting work to share today—excerpts from a new novel in progress, and a poetry reading by Violet Scott—I'm sure we will all enjoy Violet's poems as we always do. And of course we'll have open time for others who want to read.'

Shelby stifled a groan. Mark sent her a sideways look that accused her of wasting his time. This could go on for hours, he seemed to be saying.

I can't believe I'm sitting still for this, she thought as waves of generalistic, high-toned poetry rolled over the room in Violet Scott's deep voice. Of course, Shelby thought wearily, the woman would have to be a poet— and a lousy one at that.

But if Violet was Valerie, trying to hide—of course she wouldn't bring out her best work now. She'd been forewarned, after all, that Shelby would be at the meeting. She'd had time to prepare herself.

And if she got back to New York with her mind in one piece after all this confusion, Shelby thought wearily, she would never set a foot west of Philadelphia again. It was hazardous to her mental health!

Mark stirred beside her as if he were uncomfortable,

and put his arm across the back of her chair. Shelby could sympathise with his discomfort; the chairs were hard and small. But she felt just a little restless herself at being claimed so nonchalantly, and when he casually stroked the nape of her neck under the upswept hair, she felt as if an icicle had been rubbed over her spine. It must look to every woman in the room as if they were lovers, she thought resentfully.

And, had it not been for the hotel manager, she admitted, they would have been. For an instant, Shelby found herself regretting that ill-timed intrusion the night before. What would it have been like? she wondered idly. Was he a gentle lover, or—— Horrified at the direction her thoughts were taking, she dragged her mind back to the poetry.

But eventually Violet's masterpiece drew to a close and the excerpt from the novel, which the author insisted would be a new classic in horror fiction, was behind them. The babble broke out again as the horde of women headed for the tea-table. There had been not a word of acknowledgment about Shelby's presence or her reasons for being there.

I wasted a whole afternoon of my precious time on this? she thought, and then told herself to think on the positive side. At least Rodney wasn't in town to complicate her life, and her search for Valerie.

The president came towards Shelby. 'I'm so sorry about not introducing you to the meeting,' she said. 'But a few of our members were uncomfortable with having an editor here, and felt that our club would be misused if we were to be drawn into a search for a particular author.'

That roughly translated, Shelby thought, meant that Violet Scott didn't want her to come. It was no surprise to her; the woman had made no secret of her opposition last night. But it did make Shelby wonder if Patricia Buchanan had been right.

Mark seemed to have read her mind. 'The lady in question doth protest quite a little,' he misquoted blandly.

'But I mentioned to several of the key members that you'd be here,' the president went on, 'and they were delighted to offer any help they can. I wondered, in fact, if you'd like to stop by my house this evening. We can relax and talk about it—perhaps I can help.'

'That would be wonderful,' Shelby smiled.

'Good. I've invited some people to drop in—instinct says they will know if anyone would.' She pressed a visiting card into Shelby's hand. 'Snacks and things— seven o'clock—make Mark bring you.' She smiled and was off to join another group.

'Mark has made other plans,' he pointed out. 'And after the waste of time this afternoon has been, I'd really like to accomplish something today.'

'That was like a royal command, wasn't it? Well, you don't have to go,' Shelby told him. Disappointment washed over her. It came as a shock; after all, she was a big girl. She didn't need to hold on to Mark's hand all the time. But, she wondered a little jealously, just what was he planning to do?

He sighed. 'I don't have a choice. She lives miles out of town—you can't possibly hitchike. Besides, Shelby, you're so innocent that you'll believe anything they tell you. For all you know, the president herself is Valerie St. Swithin's Day.'

'St. John!' she snapped, suddenly losing patience with him.

'Whatever,' Mark shrugged. 'She might just be fiendishly clever.'

'What's so clever about inviting me into her house?'

'She wants to find out what course your investigation is taking,' he pointed out patiently, 'to discover whether you're hot on her trail or still totally lost. And to feed you false clues——'

'You're a damned cynic, Mark Buchanan.'

'And you are a hopeless romantic. It makes us a wonderful team—don't you think?' He tucked her hand into his elbow and smiled down into her eyes, and Shelby promptly forgot that she was irritated with him. It isn't fair, she thought, that a man can be so damned handsome and charming too. The whole feminine half of the population is in danger whenever he's around.

Especially me, she thought. Especially me.

CHAPTER EIGHT

'WHAT now?' Mark said as they left the bedlam of the writers' club meeting. They could still hear the high-pitched voices out on the street, and Shelby waited till they were almost back to Patricia's house before she answered.

'The library again, I suppose. I want to look at that local history room. But you don't have to trail along——'

He grinned. 'Be honest, Shel. You want me to be there, don't you?' He opened the gate in Patricia's white picket fence and ushered Shelby through.

She looked up into his dark, amused eyes, and whispered, 'Yes.' And she knew that she was giving him a great deal more than an invitation to come along to the library.

He knew it too. He drew a short, sharp breath, and pulled her into his arms; it was a gesture without gentleness, but Shelby didn't mind. The hard contact of his body, the strength of his arms holding her, felt right and natural. From some distant corner of her mind, however, conscience warned, and she murmured, 'Shouldn't we go inside? Kissing on the front steps, for heaven's sake——'

Mark's voice was rough. 'If we go inside we won't stop with a kiss, Shelby. Not this time. That's a promise.'

I feel different about him to the way I have about any other man in my life, she thought dreamily, and her fingers wandered through the curly hair at the back of his neck as he kissed her.

There had been men in her life, and plenty of them,

but they had been brief passing relationships, and she hadn't fooled herself into thinking that she was really in love. Most of the time, she thought, she'd been far more intrigued by the idea of falling in love than with the particular man involved, and usually as soon as he made a move to get serious, Shelby had backed away.

Perhaps it was silly, she had told herself over the years as she watched her friends go from one affair to the next, that she didn't want to live as they did. After all, what was wrong with having fun? It didn't seem to hurt anyone.

But something deep inside Shelby resisted the idea of easy affairs and casual sex. There had to be more to love than that, she had told herself, and she didn't want to settle for less than the best.

And now, she thought hazily, her senses reeling under the sensual assault of Mark's kiss, she was standing here on Patricia Buchanan's front steps, kissing him as if he'd just come home from the war. And she was ready to throw all those old ideas away and go to bed with a man she'd known for only a few days . . .

But it was different, she told herself, trying to make sense out of her jumbled emotions. Mark was different. It wasn't just a physical attraction she was feeling, as it had been with many of those other men. And she wasn't so unrealistic as to expect Mark to be perfection. Even when he was cool and cynical and sarcastic, she still wanted him—those things were part of him. She wanted much more than a sexual relationship with him—she wanted to share his most secret thoughts, his fears, his laughter, his sorrows.

And if that isn't love, she thought humbly, then I'll probably never know what love is . . .

Mark raised his head, and his voice had a ragged edge to it as he said, 'The library. Did you say something about the library?'

Reality returned, if only hazily, to Shelby. She was in Warren's Grove for a purpose, after all, and she wasn't going to find Valerie unless she continued to look. 'Right,' she said regretfully.

Laughter sparkled in his dark eyes. 'Unless you'd rather go inside after all——'

'Mark, I don't think your Aunt Pat would approve.' Shelby tucked loose strands of hair back into the upswept knot and wished that she had a mirror. She suspected that even the most casual observer would have no trouble in recognising that she had just been thoroughly kissed.

'We could go to the hotel instead,' he pointed out.

'I know darn well the manager wouldn't approve. Come on, we've only got a little time before the library closes,' she cajoled.

Mark sighed. 'Slave-driver,' he muttered, and tucked her hand into his elbow. His arm brushed ever so casually against her breast, and his expression dared her to protest.

The librarian looked up with suspicion in her eyes, and Shelby wished even more that she had managed a look into a mirror. Had her lipstick ended up all over her face? Was her hair straggling around her head like a witch's twig broom?

'Hello, Miss Branch,' Mark told her cheerfully. 'We'd like to look through the local history room, please.'

The librarian eyed Shelby with distate. 'I'll be closing in half an hour,' she said firmly.

'It will take us only twenty minutes or so,' Mark countered.

Shelby was glad that she wasn't the one who was opposing Mark in this battle of wills. She could see the struggle on the librarian's face as she calculated the result if she refused his request. Then the woman seemed to wither. 'Come this way,' she said, and led them behind the circulation desk and through her office.

Shelby looked around the office curiously. The desk was an old-fashioned rolltop, and Shelby would bet that it was closed neatly every night at closing time. No haphazard piles of mail and notes here, she saw. A ream of plain white bond paper was so carefully stacked on the corner of the desk that Shelby was certain she could see the edge of each page. Every pigeonhole was neatly labelled, and the papers in it were arranged for easy access. The pencils were sharpened to perfect points. The blotter was as straight and clean as if it had been brand new, and on it lay a single sheet of paper with what looked like an agenda typed on it. For the next official meeting of the library board, Shelby wondered—or was it Miss Branch's personal plans for the evening?

The librarian took a key from the ring at her belt and unlocked a door. 'Twenty minutes, mind you,' she said, and Shelby fully expected her to shake a finger in Mark's face.

The air in the history room was hot and moist, and it smelled of ink and ancient paper. Books were packed together on the shelves and overflowed into stacks on the floor, and the leather bindings of the oldest ones were beginning to crumble, Shelby saw.

'Rotten shame, isn't it?' Mark said. He brushed a gentle finger across an old binding. 'Some of these things can never be replaced. They ought to be microfilmed, and then the originals should be put away in a vault where heat and humidity levels are controlled. Instead, they don't even air-condition this room—just the ones where staff members work.'

'Your Aunt Pat should know better,' Shelby chided.

'She does. It breaks her heart—but she's only one member of a board that is horrified by the high cost of air conditioning.' He frowned, and then shook off the problem. 'We can't do anything about it today, at any rate. Here's the section of local authors' stuff. I assume that's what you wanted?'

'That's it.' Shelby pulled up a stool and started to run her fingers over the titles. 'There are so many—I don't know where to start looking with just twenty minutes to work.'

'You'll have to rely on woman's intuition, I suppose.'

There were a dozen shelves, packed to bursting with books of all descriptions. 'I wouldn't have thought such a little town could have produced so many writers.'

Mark frowned. 'Anyone with a local connection gets dragged in here. They even talked me into donating a complimentary copy of each book, and I'm not even a regular resident, much less a native. But Miss Branch asked me about it so often that it finally wore me down.' He paused and pulled a volume off the shelf. 'I don't imagine you're interested in reading the repair manual for a farm tractor they once manufactured here?'

'No, thanks. Wait, could the author possibly be Valerie?'

He checked the copyright date. 'Not unless she's at least a hundred and twenty years old.'

'Then I'll pass.' Shelby was deep into the biography section, assessing each title and author's name. If Valerie had written anything besides romances she, like Mark, might have donated a copy of her work to the library. And if Shelby could just put her hands on that book, she was certain that she would recognise Valerie's distinctive writing style. Her use of words, her way of constructing a sentence, would stand out, Shelby thought; she couldn't have changed that. If Shelby could just reach into these crammed shelves and pull out a book of Valerie's—if such a thing even existed. That was the real frustration, she admitted.

'*Warren's Grove: A Family Devoted*,' she read off the spine of a large, leatherbound book. 'By Patricia Buchanan. Mark, it's your Aunt Pat's book!'

He raised an eyebrow. 'Do you expect me to be surprised? Miss Branch got to her too. That woman is like water torture—she never quits.'

Shelby pulled it off the shelf. 'This is a beautiful cover, Mark. It must have cost her a fortune to have this bound.'

'Aunt Pat doesn't do anything halfway.' He sounded preoccupied. 'Here's one called *Love on the Plains*——That might be Valerie,' He glanced at the title page. 'Oh, sorry. It's a diary of a covered wagon trip instead.'

Shelby gave him credit. 'It was a nice try. Lora Wilde would probably adore that one,' she added. 'She would think of it as modern mid-western realism.' She opened Pat's book to the large photograph in the front. It was a stiff, formal portrait of an early member of the Warren family, and she looked from it to Mark and shook her head. 'No resemblance at all,' she said. 'You have that lean and hungry look, and he——'

'Why do you think I look lean and hungry anyway?' Mark challenged. 'That ancestor of mine didn't have to deal with modern women. If he wanted a girl, all he had to do was to pick her up, throw her over the pommel of his saddle and drag her home. Modern man gets frustrated instead, while he waits around for the girl to make up her mind.'

'Poor baby,' Shelby cooed. 'Why don't you try his methods some time and see what happens?'

'I'd end up in jail,' Mark grumbled. 'Besides, I don't own a saddle. Why are you wasting your library time on Pat's book, anyway? There's a copy up at the house if you're really interested in the Warrens.'

Shelby smiled. 'Don't you want me to read what she has to say about you? Does she tell all about your early escapades?—I'm certain there were a great many.'

'You have less than five minutes left, Shel,' he warned.

She put the book back. 'All right, all right. I'll read it tomorrow at the house.'

'You promised to paint tomorrow,' Mark countered.

'Did I?' Shelby looked up with innocently wide eyes. 'My goodness, I must see a doctor about these memory lapses I'm having.'

'I should have known you'd try to weasel out of it somehow,' he grumbled. 'You're going to keep your promise, dear heart, if I have to use you for the paintbrush.'

The librarian came to the door. 'Your time is up,' she announced coldly. 'Did you find what you were looking for?'

'Not really,' Mark said. 'We'll have to come back tomorrow.'

The librarian froze a little more still. Just what was her problem? Shelby wondered. Did she think of every item in the building as her personal property?

'We're still checking up on the local authors,' Mark continued, ignoring the glacial treatment he was getting. 'We just came from the writers' club, as a matter of fact.'

'Oh, yes, the writers.' The librarian's tone was cool. 'They used to meet here, in our conference room.'

'Used to?' Shelby questioned. 'It sounds like an ideal arrangement, with all the research material right here——'

'You'd think so,' the librarian sniffed, 'but we had to put a stop to it. They were far too rowdy.'

Mark managed to turn his strangled chuckle into an uncontrollable cough. Shelby glared at him for a moment, and then the humour of the comment overtook her too. Noisy the club meeting had certainly been, but the librarian's phrase had left Shelby with the mental image of a group of women climbing the shelves, tearing pages from books to fold into paper aeroplanes, and doing a frantic polka across the tables.

She fled the library and gave in to a fit of giggles on the front steps. Mark followed, and behind them the lock clicked heavily as the librarian, with the look of heavy suspicion still shuttering her face, closed the building for another day.

'I hate to tell you this,' Mark said, when he had finally stopped laughing, 'but you look as if you've just come down from cleaning out the attic. Dust doesn't go well with a white suit, though I think the streak on your nose is kind of cute.'

'Darn!' Shelby tried in vain to brush the dirt off her jacket.

'And don't blame me,' he added. 'I wanted to go to the hotel before we came here, but you said no.'

'Well, we'll have to go back now,' she said.

Mark grinned. 'Oh, good.'

'And don't get any ideas!'

'Well, at least not any new ones,' he agreed.

She didn't invite him up to her room, but he came anyway. Shelby tugged an orchid trouser suit out of her suitcase and started for the bathroom to change, muttering under her breath about people who were so thoughtless that they put other people to great amounts of unnecessary trouble.

Mark, who had flung himself across her bed, looked up with eyes sparkling. 'You don't have to go to any trouble,' he advised, 'you can change right here. I'll close my eyes or something, if you're shy.'

'Sorry, Mark. I don't trust you.' She clicked the bathroom door shut.

'How are you doing with this pile of manuscripts?' he called. 'Have you read them all?'

'About half. And I haven't found six well-written sentences in the whole half-million words either.'

'Perseverance, dear heart,' he recommended.

'I'm about to give up on it. I've spent too much time as it is reading it instead of looking for Valerie.'

There was a long silence, and then Mark said, 'Are you certain you want to quit?'

Shelby tucked her bright printed blouse into the waistband of her slacks and opened the door. 'Of course I'm certain. What's the matter with you?'

Mark shrugged. He looked extremely comfortable, stretched out on the bed with his hands folded behind his head. 'It occurs to me—from my reading of her letters—that Valerie San Francisco——'

'San Francisco?' Shelby could hardly believe her ears.

'So? What's wrong with that? It was named for a saint, and I'm running low on them.'

'Where are you getting all of these ridiculous names?'

'I go home every night and read my *Encyclopedia Britannica*. At any rate, the lady in question has an odd sense of what is funny. Am I right?'

Shelby nodded. 'Absolutely. Her sense of humour is extremely dry. Why?'

'I think it would tickle her sense of the ridiculous to have slipped you something. An early manuscript, perhaps—just to see if you would catch it.'

'That's a little far out, Mark.' She sat down on the edge of the bed and reached for an envelope that lay precariously on the edge of the night table. 'Take this one for example——'

He made a face. 'Must I take it?'

'You don't want it, that's sure,' Shelby admitted. 'I don't think Valerie would do anything of the sort.'

'But if she did,' Mark said solemnly, 'she's sitting somewhere laughing at you right now.'

Shelby thought it over. Much as she hated to admit it, Mark was right. It was the kind of thing Valerie might do. If, she reminded herself, Valerie was still in town, and if she was in any mood to find this search funny, she might have done something of the sort as a prank.

'I wish I'd asked them to open that letter,' she mused.

'What letter?'

'Oh, didn't I tell you?' Shelby had honestly forgotten.

'I called the office this morning. I got a letter from Valerie this week.'

Mark looked as if she'd hit him with a hammer. A long moment later he said, unbelievingly, 'And you didn't have them open it? What kind of nut are you?'

'Don't yell at me,' Shelby protested. 'I didn't dare have them read it. Nobody but me knows that she quit.'

Mark groaned. 'Why don't we just give the whole thing up?' he asked. 'Call them tomorrow morning and have them read you the letter. Maybe then we could spend the rest of the week having a little fun instead of chasing after a shadow——'

'But what if she's angry?' Shelby's voice held a painful intensity. 'What if that letter tells me to leave her alone? You can't keep that sort of news quiet in a publishing house. It will go straight to my boss, and I'd be fired instantly.'

'Not if you aren't there,' Mark pointed out.

'Obviously you don't know Bob Jonas! He'd send me a registered letter, and that would be the end of it. No, Mark, I don't dare take the chance. And in the meantime we might still find Valerie before Saturday. We might even be introduced to her tonight. The letter will have to wait till I get back.'

He looked her over thoughtfully, shook his head, and smiled. It was a slow, warm smile, and it surprised Shelby; she had expected that he would be harder to convince.

But she wasn't going to chance starting the argument all over again by questioning what he was thinking. 'Speaking of letters, did you check Valerie's mailbox today? I haven't been down there.'

'Your note is still there. Nothing else, though.'

'Darn. I wonder if she has gone away for a while,' Shelby mused. She opened another envelope. This manuscript wasn't even typed; it was handwritten in lavender ink on lined notebook paper. That one would be easy enough to respond to.

She looked over at Mark, who had closed his eyes as if he was drifting off for a nap. 'Why don't you help read these manuscripts,' she asked, 'if you're so sure that it needs to be done?'

Mark shook his head. 'I've only skimmed Valerie St. Ignatius Loyola's books, which hardly makes me an authority on her style.'

'It's no challenge to tell the difference between genuinely bad stuff and what comes out when a good writer tries very hard to write bad stuff,' Shelby said. She got her glasses from the night-table and pulled another manuscript out of the envelope.

'If you hate this so much, how do you manage to stay sane on the job?'

'Because everything is screened before I get it. I never have to see the really bad stuff.' She propped herself up with the pillows and started to read.

Mark had moved so quietly that she was startled when he put an arm around her waist and drew her down on to the bed beside him. 'It seems to me there is a very fine line between the two. Now if you'd like to do something fun——'

'I thought you wanted me to read manuscripts. Mark——'

'Not now, darling.' He was nibbling her earlobe.

'Mark—I'm trying to get this done.'

'Ummm, so am I. Put the book down, honey.'

She clung to it as if it were armour, 'Mark, you're smearing up my lenses.'

'That's easy to solve.' He put her glasses back on the table and kissed her eyelids.

She said, a little shakily, 'Don't you think we should have a sandwich or something before we go out to that party?'

'Aren't you interested in anything but food?' he murmured against her throat. 'You're going to get fat.'

'You're the one who's always hungry.' She could

already hear the answer to that, and so she plunged on. 'I just thought—we don't want to be late——'

Mark smiled down at her, and the top button of her blouse slid free. His hand slipped casually into the gap and down over the satin skin to cup her breast. 'We have plenty of time. Besides, when she says snacks, she means that there will be enough food for the whole state to drop in.'

'But we're supposed to be finding Valerie——'

'I do my best creative thinking when my hands are busy. Remember?' His long fingers tugged at another button.

'Mark, quit it! We're due at a party in half an hour——'

'So let's have our own party right here instead. Let Valerie St John the Baptist go to the devil. It's what you want to do.'

She tried to push him away. 'What do you mean by that?'

'I mean that I'd like to have her head on a platter just now, and I think you would too. The woman is a blasted nuisance.'

'But——' If it hadn't been for Valerie, she thought, I'd never have known you . . .

He kissed her, roughly. 'Why are you lying here in my arms, Shelby?'

'Because you won't take no for an answer!'

Mark shook his head. 'Oh no, dear. That's a long way from the truth—I could force you to stay on this bed, but I'm not holding you down. So why are you here? Come to that, why didn't you just hightail it back to New York this morning when they told you about the letter?'

'Because I'm already here, and I might as well stay and look for Valerie as I'd planned to do. On Monday I'll——'

'You're lying to yourself,' he said, very softly. But

there was a hard note in his voice, a strength that sent a shiver down Shelby's spine.

'Of course I wanted to hear what the letter said this morning,' she began, 'but——'

Mark shook his head. 'Not good enough, Shelby.'

'I really did think about going back to New York today,' she said defensively, 'so I could read it for myself. But it would have been like burning my bridges. If the letter didn't tell me who she was I would have lost my last chance to find her. I wouldn't have time then to come back——'

'Oh, all those things are true,' he said coolly, 'but that's not the reason you stayed.'

'Then what is?' Shelby challenged. 'If you're so smart, why don't you tell me?'

Mark seemed not to have heard her. He nibbled at her throat, letting his lips travel slowly up from the pulse point in the hollow at the bottom until he reached her chin. 'If you can't figure that one out, dear heart, you needn't think I'm going to help you,' he said softly.

For a long moment she stared up into his eyes, trying to decide if he was laughing at her or deadly serious. Then he rolled away from her and on to his feet, and stretched a hand down to pull her off the bed.

'Time to go,' he said. 'You'd hate it if I explained to our hostess precisely why we're late.'

She was furious. First he said he didn't want to go at all, then he blamed her for their being late! The man was hopeless. But his question was still nagging at her as they drove through the quiet darkness on their way to the party. Mark didn't say a word, and Shelby was too absorbed in her thoughts to notice.

Why *hadn't* she taken the first plane back to New York? She could have been in the office by now, and perhaps the mystery would have been solved. There was an even chance that Valerie's letter would tell her where the woman was—who she was. But Shelby hadn't seriously considered leaving Warren's Grove until her week was up.

Then the answer hit her. *I stayed*, she thought miserably, *because I didn't want to leave you, Mark. Because I never want to leave you at all.*

Love, she thought miserably. I've tried to joke it away, since the idea first came to me last night. But this is no joke, and it's no infatuation. This is for ever.

CHAPTER NINE

THEIR hostess was at the door of her cedar-shingled house, waiting for them. Light spilled from the big windows, bright against the half-twilight outside. Mark parked his car at the end of the drive and came around to open Shelby's door.

He hadn't said a word since they had left the hotel, and it was beginning to bother her. It wasn't like Mark to be moodily silent, and Shelby wondered what was bothering him. She put her hand into his, and looked up into his eyes.

'Mark——'

His jaw was clenched, she saw, as if he was angry. *With me?* she wondered. *Understandable, if so. He called me a tease once, and that's how I must look to him.*

'Shel,' he said slowly, 'I'm probably all kinds of fool not to have asked this before now, but . . .'

She waited, almost afraid to breathe for fear that he would retreat into that unaccustomed silence again.

'It didn't even occur to me. Is there a husband waiting for you back in New York?' He sounded almost shy, like a little boy bringing flowers to his first girlfriend.

It might be twilight outside, but Shelby's world was suddenly bathed in sunshine. 'No one,' she said, very softly. 'No one at all, Mark.'

'I was beginning to be afraid,' he confessed. 'Afraid that you were pretending that you were attracted to me, just to keep me interested in the search for Valerie——'

He wasn't even touching her, but the warmth of his eyes was like a caress. Shelby felt absolutely transparent, certain that he could see her deepest secrets now. And she didn't mind a bit. 'Valerie who?' she said, a little unsteadily.

He smiled, a long, slow, sensual smile that made Shelby want to melt into a puddle in his arms and never, never move.

'I know why I stayed, now,' she admitted. 'You were right, Mark.' The tone of her voice was a promise.

'It's darn shame you didn't find that out before we got here,' he scolded. 'We're stuck for the evening. I don't think she'll accept excuses now.'

Shelby glanced over his shoulder at the hostess, still waiting in the doorway. 'You're right. It's too late.'

'No,' he corrected, 'not too late for us, Shelby. Just postponed, that's all.' He took her hand with a newly possessive attitude, tucked it into his elbow so that he could hold her close to his side, and led her towards the house.

There were people everywhere. The sole topic of discussion seemed to be Valerie; her name echoed from room to room. Shelby was no sooner inside the door than she was surrounded by a chattering group, some with faces that were vaguely familiar from the afternoon's meeting, and each with a theory about Valerie. Another group surrounded Mark, and the two of them were soon separated. It felt, Selby thought, like being left adrift in a raging sea, surrounded by sharks, with her lifeboat—Mark—vanishing in the distance.

'Is Patricia home from her seminar yet?' she heard someone ask him. 'I hope she'll teach another class at the college this winter. I have some things I'd really like her to see. Or maybe—do you think Miss Stuart might have time?'

Shelby saw Mark smile and shake his head. 'Shelby's very busy,' he said, and she turned her attention to the group around her. Sweet of Mark, she thought, and then smiled to herself. Not sweet at all, actually, she decided. Mark was simply protecting her free time so he could have it. It made her feel warm and sheltered.

'You know,' remarked one of the women. 'I think it's mighty suspicious that Violet wouldn't come tonight. I asked her, and so did Madge. But she just put her snooty nose up in the air and——'

'Oh, Violet's just jealous,' said another. 'If anyone came to town trying to buy her poetry, she'd be standing on his doorstep the next morning. She just doesn't want anyone else to succeed. Now I think——'

The hostess put a tall glass of pineapple juice in Shelby's hand. She smiled gratefully, took a long drink, and turned her attention back to the group.

'I think you should ask at the school,' said one woman. 'Maybe it's someone in the English department there.'

'The whole thing is silly, anyway,' said a third. 'Anyone can write those things. No offence, Miss Stuart, but it's true.'

'If it's so easy, then why don't you do it?' one of the other women said cattily.

The sceptic ignored her. 'What's the big deal about finding this woman? How important can one writer be to a big publishing house, anyway?' She turned to Shelby. 'I think it's all a gimmick you dreamed up,' she accused.

There has to be one in every crowd, Shelby thought, Days of exposure to Mark's brand of cynicism made her wonder if the protester might herself be Valerie.

'I think we need some organisation here,' announced another woman. 'We need a list of everyone who might fit the pattern, and then we can start eliminating suspects.'

'What do you think you're doing, investigating a murder?' another objected. 'She hasn't committed any crime. Maybe the woman just wants some privacy!'

I'm beginning to understand why Valerie didn't make a

public announcement, Shelby thought. *She knows this little town very well indeed.*

'She's a public treasure!' another said. 'We should put up a billboard at the edge of town and let everybody know we have our own celebrity.'

And if Valerie was here, Shelby thought wearily, and overheard that line of reasoning, she would never write another word for fear of being caught! For the first time she began to understand what she had done by coming to Warren's Grove at all. From now on, whenever a book bearing Valerie St John's name on it hit the racks, these people would be tearing it to shreds, searching for clues. They would be sneaking looks at the woman behind the counter or the one who was pushing the shopping cart, wondering all the time, *Is she Valerie?*

And for all this, Shelby told herself solemnly, you *are responsible. If you think she's going to pop up at the door of your hotel room with a cheerful smile and announce who she is, you're crazy, Shelby Stuart! Whoever this woman is, she is certainly no fool.*

Valerie was there, she thought suddenly. She was in this room—she could feel her presence. It was almost as if a shadow had fallen across her path, and if Shelby could just turn her head fast enough, she would be able to see Valerie——

'You can speculate all you want,' said a little woman who had just joined the group. Nora, Shelby thought, the one who had insisted last night at the country club that she had found Valerie. 'All you're doing is guessing,' the woman went on, 'but I know who she is.'

The others scoffed, but Shelby caught Nora's eye across the group. 'I'm glad you came tonight,' she said. 'I wanted to talk to you this afternoon, but you were so busy with your guests that I didn't get the chance.'

Nora smiled. 'I should have known how it would turn out,' she said. 'Once Violet has made up her mind about something, no one else can bend her decree.'

'So who is it?' one of the others asked. 'If you're so sure, Nora——'

Nora smiled. 'I didn't think much of it when it happened,' she said. 'It did seem a little odd at the time, but it wasn't until Miss Stuart started asking about Valerie St John that I even remembered it.'

'Do you think it's Violet?' Shelby quizzed quietly.

Nora's eyes flashed. 'Heavens, no! Violet's just envious; they're right about that. Valerie St John is really Mary Branch.'

A dead silence dropped over the room. It was a stillness so complete that when a man across the room dropped a radish it sounded like a bowling ball bouncing across the floor.

Mary Branch? Shelby thought, dazed. Did she mean Miss Branch?

Then someone giggled, and soon the entire room was full of laughter. Nora's face was red. Shelby felt a little sorry for her. However silly the suggestion might end up to be, it had been made in good faith.

'The librarian?' Shelby asked, and Nora nodded.

There was no doubt in the woman's mind, Shelby realised, and suddenly it all came together to make a crazy sort of sense. Miss Branch had checked out the books on African art and gourmet cooking, and she certainly fitted what Valerie had said about working in a library.

I knew this all came back to the library, Shelby thought. *I knew it instinctively, and I just didn't follow the trail quite closely enough.* All those nasty things Miss Branch had said about romances, and the people who write them, and the publishers—it could have all been a bluff, a cover-up.

And so much for her ideas about being psychic, Shelby told herself rudely. Valerie here in this room— indeed!

'Sure,' said one of the more suspicious listeners, 'and

I'm the tooth fairy, too. What makes you think that Miss Branch ever wrote anything sexier than a letter to her little sister?'

Shelby drained her pineapple juice, and someone put another glass in her hand.

'Because I stopped there one day to renew my books,' Nora said, sounding important. 'It was early, before opening hours, actually, but she'd unlocked the door. When I went in, she was sorting out reams and reams of paper on the circulation desk. I couldn't read what was on it, but it was all typed, double-spaced and everything, and if it wasn't a manuscript I'll eat it.'

'Want some salt and pepper? It was probably just her annual report to the board; it's as long as a novel sometimes.'

'If it was a library project,' Nora asked sweetly, 'why was she sorting it into big manilla envelopes? And why did she scramble it into a pile and push it into a drawer as soon as she realised I was there?'

It was a telling argument. One of the women nodded. 'It makes sense,' she admitted. 'Miss Branch never treats a piece of paper with anything but respect. If she was shoving pages into a drawer, she must have had a reason.'

'And——' Nora paused for dramatic effect. 'She turned fiery red when she saw me, and she stumbled around and stammered as if she'd been caught behind the desk half-undressed.'

There were a few murmurs and nods. Shelby wasn't paying attention. She had closed her eyes and was trying to picture Miss Branch's office in her mind. The big roll-top desk, the agenda lying neatly in the centre of the blotter—— Yes, there had been manilla envelopes, several of them, in one of the pigeonholes. Not an unusual item for a librarian to have, of course, but there nonetheless. And on the corner of the desk had been a neat stack of white bond paper.

Would Miss Branch have left a couple of hundred sheets of blank paper lying loose on the corner of her desk? Shelby asked herself. Wouldn't someone as compulsively neat as Miss Branch either put the paper in a drawer or leave it in the wrapper until it was used, rather than risk getting the edges bent up?

Probably she would, if the paper was blank. But if it was her own copy of a manuscript——

'Valerie told me that she had worked in a library,' Shelby muttered under her breath, as if trying the idea out. Then, with a dawning certainty that this was the answer, she went on, 'I assumed, from the way she said it, that she no longer did. But it was phrased in such a way that it could also have meant she had worked there for years.'

Her initial excitement was beginning to die down. The first thrill of discovery, of winning this impossible game she had set herself, was dissipating.

Valerie, she thought sadly, and mourned for the golden girl of her imagination. It was only now, as she tried to adjust her mind to the idea of Miss Branch, that she realised how completely she had pictured Valerie in her mind. She should have been blonde, Shelby thought painfully. Tall, slim, and elegant, and very, very blonde. She should be married, too—to a handsome professional man who adored her, who brought her flowers and kissed her hand and made love to her every night till dawn . . .

But Miss Branch? Shelby's soul shivered away from the idea.

Besides, she thought drearily as she moved towards the punch-bowl and refilled her glass, Miss Branch had left her with little hope for the future. After what the librarian had said, Shelby was certain that this newly-discovered Valerie would not be easily talked into writing any more romances for Jonas Brothers. She'd have to ask her, of course, tomorrow morning. But Shelby wasn't going to hold her breath about the result.

Mark found her beside the punch-bowl. 'Miss Branch? I can't believe that.' He was still shaking his head.

'It makes sense, Mark. She was so nervous today when we were in the library that I wondered what on earth could be wrong.'

'It still doesn't seem possible.' He was frowning a little.

'Did you see the stack of paper on her desk? It could have been a manuscript.'

'No, I missed it. Of course, it could have been a dozen other things instead,' he warned. He reached for a plate and started to load it with tiny sandwiches, pickles, chips. 'What are you going to do, Shelby?'

Shelby filled her glass with punch and yawned. 'I suppose I'll go talk to her. Confront her with what I know——'

'That's just what I mean. What do you *know*? You have some evidence, but as far as proving anything——' A look of horror crossed his face as she drank half of her punch in a gulp. 'How much of that stuff have you had?' he demanded.

'I don't know. It's good—try it. I'm very thirsty, for some reason.'

Mark swallowed hard. 'Have you had anything to eat?'

Shelby shook her head. 'I'm not hungry after all. Just disappointed, and tired.' She yawned again. 'I don't know what's got into me—I can't keep my eyes open all of a sudden. It must be the relief of having the puzzle solved——'

'On the other hand, it might be the damned punch,' Mark said tartly. He set his plate down and tried to take the glass from her hand.

'What's the matter with you? I'm just drinking pineapple juice, Mark.'

'Oh, is that all? You must not be aware that the brew you're slugging down is known around Warren's Grove as Passion Punch—because after three glasses of it, you're either kissing someone you've never met before or you're ready to step outside to fight him.'

Shelby held up the glass and inspected it. 'Are you telling me this is partly alcohol?' She was having a little trouble thinking about what he was saying, she noticed.

'I'd guess the proportions at about half, dear heart. I wonder which category you'll fit into,' he mused as he took her arm. 'Are you a lover or a fighter? At any rate, we're going home, Shel. Right now, before you make a fool of yourself.'

'But I don't want to——' Defiantly, she finished off the glass of punch before she let Mark take it out of her hand. 'Stop spoiling my party, Mark.' The words suddenly wouldn't come out straight.

As he put her into the front seat of his car, he said, 'I can tell that we got here not a minute too soon.'

'Let's stop and talk to Miss Branch tonight,' she suggested merrily.

'Let's wait till morning.'

'I was right after all,' she crowed. 'I said someone had to know who Valerie is. And someone did!'

'Why don't you put your head back and rest till we get home?' Mark recommended.

But Shelby already had. She had curled up in the bucket seat, her hand propped under her chin, her hair falling over her face. 'I haven't been so relaxed in ages,' she murmured, and went to sleep. It was fortunate for her that she couldn't hear what Mark was muttering under his breath.

She came to consciousness slowly and reluctantly, afraid to move, and began to take stock. It was morning; that was definite, for sunshine spilled in through the window panes, filtered by sheer curtains. And it was just as obvious that she wasn't at the hotel, for the windows of her room there faced west.

Therefore if she wasn't in her own bed——

She turned her head very slowly, afraid that a sharp movement might make it fall off, to confirm her suspicions. 'Oh, my God!' she moaned, when she saw Mark's dark head on the pillow next to hers. She would have screamed if she hadn't been afraid that it would make her headache worse.

It's not fair, she told herself. It wasn't as if she had intended to drink herself into oblivion last night. She wasn't used to alcohol; she couldn't take its effects. And just how, she wondered, could she bring herself to ask Mark if she'd had a good time after they got home?

Oh, God, you've really done it this time, she told herself. *If you're going to sleep with somebody, Shelby, it would be nice if you at least remembered what it was like!*

Her mouth tasted like dried wallpaper paste. How, she wondered vaguely, was it possible that something so pleasant as the pineapple punch could leave such an awful aftertaste?

Mark stirred, stretched, and turned to look at her. Shelby closed her eyes and pretended to be asleep.

'You're not quite fast enough, darling,' he said, and kissed the corner of her mouth. 'No playing possum this morning. How do you feel?'

'Lousy,' Shelby muttered.

Mark laughed. 'You do know why they call it intoxication, don't you?'

'You're heartless to laugh at a sick woman. And I don't really care what they call it.'

'It's because alcohol is actually poisonous—it's toxic to your system. Thus the word intoxicated. Bet you never thought of that before, did you?'

'No. And I don't plan to worry about it in the future, either. If I'd known what was in that stuff—I haven't been drunk in years, Mark.'

'You certainly made up for it last night.'

She would have thrown something at him, but there was nothing handy. 'I don't do this kind of thing regularly, you know.'

'Oh, I believe you. I'll get you some aspirin,' he offered. 'You'll feel better in a little while.'

'I don't think I'll ever feel better.' How much of this sick feeling, she wondered, was actually a physical reaction to the alcohol, and how much was shock? What did she do last night? And what did Mark think about it?

She sneaked a sideways look at him. He'd punched his pillow up into a wad against the carved headboard of the sleigh-backed bed and was watching her through half-closed eyes. *He looks contented*, she thought bitterly. Well, that answered one question for her.

'Which did I turn out to be?' she asked. 'A lover or a fighter?'

Mark laughed. He leaned over her, propping himself up on his elbows, and kissed her, long and softly. 'Do I have a black eye?' he asked.

'Not that I can see.'

'Does that answer your question?'

Shelby pulled the pillow over her head and moaned in utter frustration. How could he do that? she asked herself furiously. How could he make love to her when he must have known she was completely out of control——?

The mattress bounced as he slid out of bed, and Shelby groaned. She kept her eyes tightly shut, afraid even to look at him. She didn't think she could bear to see that lean, muscled body of his and know that last night he had held her, kissed her, made love to her—and now she could remember none of it.

'Take a couple of aspirin, you'll feel better,' he said. He set the bottle on the night table with a click that echoed through her head. 'Want some coffee?'

'No, thanks.'

'Well, I do. I'll be back in a minute with my sure-fire hangover cure.'

She waited till his cheerful whistle had died away down the stairs, and then she sat up carefully and swallowed two tablets. After a little while her head cleared a bit, but her mouth was still dry. She pushed the blankets back and swung her feet out of bed. She was a little startled to note that she was wearing a pyjama coat, in a perfectly awful dark green plaid. She certainly didn't remember putting it on.

'Thoughtful of him,' she muttered sarcastically. 'He probably wanted to be sure I didn't catch a cold.'

She stumbled into the bathroom and rinsed her mouth, wishing she had her toothbrush. Then she said, 'The heck with it,' and borrowed Mark's. After all, she thought, they'd shared a bed. What problem could there be if she used his toothbrush?

His whistle warned her that he was climbing the stairs. She had no place to run, so she climbed hastily back into bed and propped herself up with all the pillows. Mark was going to have a few things to explain, she decided.

'You look much better,' he said. 'Your colour is coming back. I brought you some coffee after all—thought you might have changed your mind.'

She wrapped her hands around the cup, letting the warmth soak into her fingers, and tried a tentative sip. 'You said you'd bring me some crazy concoction to cure my headache,' she said.

'Yeah,' he smiled, sitting down on the edge of the bed. He was wearing the pyjama pants that matched her jacket. 'But drink your coffee first.'

'Mark,' she said uncertainly. 'About last night——'

'Yes, dear heart?'

She bit the bullet. 'Well, it's obvious that I didn't offend you, but—I need to know. What did I do?'

He watched her over the rim of his cup as he sipped coffee. 'You honestly don't remember?'

Shelby shook her head. 'Not a thing after we left the party.'

'I see.' The silence dragged out till she was ready to scream. Then he set his cup down, took hers out of her hand, and put it on the night table.

She was really in for it now, Shelby thought. Much as she resented what he'd done, she really couldn't blame him for being angry. He would hardly take it as a compliment that she couldn't remember a thing about the night . . .

He put his hands on her shoulders and pushed her gently back into the pillows. His eyes were dark and serious. 'Nothing,' he said. 'And now for my guaranteed hangover cure——'

His mouth was warm and firm against hers, gentle and yet demanding a response. Automatically, Shelby gave it, relaxing against him, her lips softening to let his tongue explore. Her love for him clamoured for fulfillment, urging that she pull him down beside her and engulf him in the raging fire that swept her body. It must have been something special last night, she thought hazily, for her body was begging for gratification.

His breathing was slightly ragged. He murmured something deep in his throat, and turned his attention to the shadowed cleavage left bare by the deep neckline of the pyjama top she wore.

'Wait a minute,' Shelby said, as realisation dawned. 'Did you just tell me that nothing happened last night?'

He didn't answer for a long moment. He was too busy with her buttons, and it wasn't until the pyjama top was pushed aside and her breasts left bare to his gaze that he answered. 'It depends on your definition of nothing—but if you mean did we make love last night, the answer is no.' His hand slid to the curve of her hip, caressing the silken skin with gentle warmth.

'Then—but you said—you let me think that I——'
She was suddenly righteously indignant.

Mark laughed. 'It wasn't very nice of me, was it? Call
it an irresistible impulse.' His hand moved gently down
her thigh, kneading her muscles.

'You should be ashamed of yourself!'

'I know, and it's really not your fault that you drank
too much. I didn't think to warn you about the yellow
peril, so that's partly my responsibility.'

'Then why didn't you tell me the truth when I asked?'
It was increasingly difficult to keep her mind on the
conversation, when Mark's hands were sending rivers of
delight over her entire body.

'Because you deserved a little pain, just to pay you
back for going to sleep on me last night.'

'Oh.' She gasped in pleasure as he bent his head to
nibble gently at her breast. 'I'm sorry.'

'You ought to be,' he growled. 'If you knew what you
did to my peace of mind last night, you would expect to
pay a much higher penalty . . .'

Her head was suddenly, gloriously clear. *I knew he
wasn't like that*, her heart carolled. *I knew he wouldn't
take advantage of me!*

He moved slightly, and suddenly she was pinned to
the bed by the length of his body. Still he hesitated, as if
unsure. 'Shelby——' he whispered.

'If you're expecting me to object to this,' she said
softly, 'you'll have a very long time to wait . . .'

CHAPTER TEN

IT was like a dream, so perfectly natural that she wondered—in the rare moments when she had enough presence of mind to think at all—why she had waited so long. For this was the way things were meant to be. She belonged in Mark's arms, responding to the fierce demands of his body, begging and pleading with every nerve, every cell, for release from this sweet agony.

He whispered something into her ear; as far as Shelby was concerned, it could have been Swahili, for she was incapable of making sense just then of anything except the raging torrent of emotion that swept them along.

When the storm was over and they lay quiet, still tangled in the sheets, Shelby said, her voice husky with passion, 'I warn you, Mark, don't touch me.'

He drew back as if she had slapped him.

'All that's left of me is ashes,' she explained, her voice low and rough. 'Touch me and I'll disappear in a little puff of dust.'

He considered that, and smiled. 'You're still far more solid than that, dear heart,' he said. 'In fact, I'd bet that I could do considerably more than touch you right now, and you wouldn't fall apart——'

The mere warmth of his voice was a caress; Shelby knew that if he so much as put a hand on her she would beg him to make love to her again. If she didn't love him so much, she thought a little vaguely, it would frighten her to death to feel this way.

'How's the headache?' he asked. His voice was a little indistinct because he was nuzzling her breast.

Shelby shivered at the contact, and pulled him down into her arms again. 'It's all gone.'

He raised his head and smiled. 'See? I told you I had a guaranteed cure for a hangover.'

'Be careful,' she said softly, 'you might tempt me to get drunk every night.'

'It works on a lot of other things, too,' he pointed out. 'For example, it's better than chicken soup for a cold.' He leaned over her for a quick kiss. 'This isn't getting the outside of this house painted,' he pointed out, suddenly businesslike. 'And you promised to help me today.'

Shelby groaned. 'I hoped you'd forget about that.'

He laughed, and offered, 'I'll flip you to see who cooks breakfast.'

'No need. You may have the honour.'

'How thoughtful of you,' he mocked. 'All right. But tomorrow is your turn.'

And all my tomorrows are yours, Shelby thought, till the end of time. She didn't say it, though. It sounded a bit maudlin, and she was just a little afraid that he might laugh at her. He had, after all, said nothing definite about the future.

When she came down after her shower, dressed in the orchid trouser suit again, he was pouring orange juice. The aroma of link sausages browning in the skillet made her mouth water. But it was the sight of Mark himself, barefoot, his hair rumpled, wearing pyjama pants and nothing else, that caught her attention.

How outrageously handsome he was, she thought as she paused in the kitchen doorway. Even the dark shadow along his unshaven jaw only added to his masculine attractiveness. Shelby stood quietly in the doorway for a few moments, admiring the play of muscles under his tanned skin as he moved about the kitchen. There was not an excess ounce of flesh anywhere on him, and her fingers itched with her desire to touch his skin. Part of her just wanted to stand there undiscovered and watch him, the other half of her longed to be in his arms again, to toy with the curly hair on his chest, to feel the strength of those muscles as he held her close.

He caught sight of her and smiled. For a moment, as his eyes roved over her body, he looked like a cat who had just finished off a whole saucer of cream.

And he's mine, she thought, with sudden pride. *All mine*.

'Can I help?' she asked lightly.

He shook his head. 'Everything's done. But I warn you that I don't plan to make a habit of this.'

'Since when is cooking breakfast a woman's work? Half and half, Mark—it's only fair.' But her heart was singing. They would be together—that was the important thing, Mark was making that much obvious. Who cared about the details? she thought.

'I suppose you're going to object to getting paint on your clothes,' he said. His gaze travelled intimately over the trim-fitting pants she was wearing, and Shelby coloured.

'I'm certainly not risking this outfit on a ladder,' she pointed out. 'It's part of my new fall wardrobe.'

He nodded. 'I thought you'd have an excuse. After breakfast, I'll hunt something out for you to wear— Aunt Pat must have an extra pair of jeans somewhere.'

'I make a wonderful cheering section,' Shelby offered. 'If you've changed your mind about having me paint, I'd be happy to stand by and hand up your brushes and things——'

He put a plate down in front of her. 'Don't plan on getting out of it,' he recommended with a smile. 'If it's fair for me to cook breakfast half the time, then you get to do half of everything else.'

Shelby shrugged. 'Yes, Master.'

'You're tempting me,' he warned as he sat down across the table from her. 'I'd like to take you back upstairs and——'

'So why don't you?' she asked demurely.

'Because you wouldn't want to explain to Aunt Pat why her house is still only half-painted—would you?'

Shelby sampled a sausage. 'I won't be here when Pat comes home. Remember?'

Mark frowned. 'Must you go back to New York?'

She felt warm, sheltered, protected. 'I only took the week off, and besides, there's the letter from Valerie. I can't let it wait any longer, even if I didn't have to be in the office on Monday.'

There was a long silence, and then Mark said crisply, 'Why don't you just call this morning and find out what the damned letter says? And tell Jonas you're taking another week's vacation while you're at it.'

Shelby made a face at him. 'Getting a little bossy, aren't we? I have to read that letter myself first; I can't afford to risk my job——'

'Wait a minute. Shelby, it's really important to me that you stay and meet Aunt Pat. I'm closer to her than I am to my own parents, for heaven's sake——'

'I've gathered that, but it's still very important to me that I talk to Valerie.'

'So trot down to the library this morning and do so.' His tone of voice brooked no argument. 'Pat will be back on Monday——'

Shelby was shaking her head. 'You were right last night, Mark. I'm just not sure enough that Miss Branch is Valerie to confront her. I'll talk to her this morning, but if she doesn't admit it, I can't accuse her. I need to read the letter first.'

His frown was beginning to look like a thundercloud. 'So use the damned telephone, Shelby.'

'Mark, you're sounding like a dictator!' Suddenly her breakfast didn't taste nearly so good. 'I suppose you think my job is just a minor hobby, and that I should drop it whenever you make plans that conflict.'

'Commuting from Florida next winter is going to be a challenge, that's sure,' he agreed.

'Perhaps I don't want to commute from Florida!' Shelby's voice was rising.

'Don't get the idea that I'll spend the winter in Connecticut,' he warned, 'and I'm certainly not moving to New York. I hate that city.'

They finished eating in silence. He had some nerve, she thought furiously, to assume that she would drop everything to go wherever he wanted—he hadn't even asked if she'd go to Florida with him!

'I'll do the dishes,' she said quietly.

'I wouldn't want you to go out of your way,' he responded with icy politeness. He pushed his chair back and left the room without another word.

Shelby's anger had cooled a little by the time the dishes were clean and put away. She supposed that Mark's assumption had been a natural one to make. After all, it wasn't exactly unusual for a woman to give up anything that stood in the way of having the man she wanted.

Especially after the way she'd behaved this morning, she thought. She'd made it pretty obvious what she wanted. *But he didn't even ask me*, she fumed. *If he had said that he wanted me to come with him, instead of just telling me that I was going to*——

Of course, she had made a few assumptions herself— among them, the idea that he would come back to New York with her. That one wasn't so very important; there was plenty of time. Whether their life together started this week or next was no big deal. But she had also assumed that because she loved him, all their disagreements would smooth themselves out so they could live happily ever after.

'Not a very realistic expectation,' she told herself, 'for a couple who plunged into an argument the very first time they exchanged words!'

Mark was apparently going to take his time showering. Shelby tapped her fingers on the arm of her chair for a few minutes, waiting for him to come down, and then started to look for a book so she could entertain herself. There was no point, she thought, in dwelling on their argument. She certainly couldn't negotiate a solution to this impasse by herself.

She tugged Patricia Buchanan's family history off the shelf. It might be wise, she thought, to know a bit about the family, and about Pat's work, After all, Mark had said that his aunt was very important to him, and Shelby wanted to make a good impression.

'When and if I get to meet her,' she told herself glumly. After that last exchange of sharp words——

What was the point of arguing, anyway? she asked herself. Her job wasn't worth losing Mark over, that was sure; by now Bob Jonas might have figured out a way to get rid of her. 'It would be foolish of you,' she muttered, 'to give up Mark for a job that may not even exist by the time you get back to the office.' There would be other jobs, other things she could do. Perhaps Mark had some ideas of his own.

An apology was in order. If, she reminded herself, Mark was willing to accept it.

At any rate, she thought, opening the book, she should at least be prepared to meet Aunt Pat, in case she and that highly-thought-of old lady ever got together.

The book startled her. It was well-organised, precise, clear—not the kind of thing she would have expected a privately-printed family history to be. In Shelby's experience, writers who paid their own publishing bills often rambled and carried on for ever, limited only by their printing budget. This was something else indeed, and she looked up at the clock half-an-hour and two chapters later in surprise that so much time had passed.

Mark had not yet come down. Was he pouting up

there? she wondered. She couldn't believe that it had
taken him so long to finding some painting clothes for
her.

Shelby called from the foot of the stairs, 'I'm going
down to the library, Mark. Back in a few minutes.'

There was a grunt from upstairs, which she
interpreted as half-hearted approval, and she closed the
door behind her with a bit of relief. If Mark was going
to be like this whenever he didn't get his way, Shelby
was glad to find it out now.

She stopped at the hotel and changed into fresh
clothes. Silly, perhaps, she told herself, but she wanted
to look her best at the library. She laughed at herself, a
little, as she fussed with the knot in the dark blue scarf
that accented her outfit. 'After all, Shelby,' she lectured
herself, 'Miss Branch has already seen you at your
worst—catty and snappy. Changing clothes won't make
a difference to her.'

She took a stack of manuscripts down to the desk.
The manager saw her, from her chair in the dining
room, and hurried out to the lobby. Relief lighted her
face. 'Miss Stuart,' she breathed. 'When you didn't
come down for breakfast, we were beginning to get
scared!'

Shelby dismissed the concern with a wave, unwilling
to explain her absence. 'I told some of these people that
they could pick up their manuscripts here,' she said. 'I
hope you don't mind. I know it's a bit of a bother, but I
didn't know what else to do with them——'

The manager cleared a space on the counter behind
the desk. 'No bother at all,' she said cheerfully. 'Did
you find any treasures?'

Shelby smiled ruefully. 'I'm afraid not. But then I
didn't come to Warren's Grove to look for a new
author, anyway—just the one I already had.'

'Yeah,' the manager said. 'It's one thing everybody
has in common. They all think they can write a book.'

The air was crisp. Down the street, someone was burning leaves; the acrid smoke added a tang to the smell of fall. In just the few days that Shelby had been in Warren's Grove, fall had settled in to stay. She shivered just a little, even with a jacket on. And by afternoon, she thought, it would be warm enough for shorts. Fall—the most surprising season. It had a different feel here to the one back East. For that, if nothing else, she was grateful. This trip had taught her that there was more to the country than the seacoast cities.

She paused in the post office to check Valerie's mailbox. Her note was still there, untouched. It looked a little lonely and bedraggled, Shelby thought, as if it knew how hopeless a task it had been given. Was Valerie hiding for a reason? she wondered, and wished again that she had asked about the postmark on that letter that awaited her in New York.

She paused at the top of the library steps and straightened her shoulders, as if she was preparing for battle. The next few minutes might bring the end of her search, she knew, if she could just find the right words with which to convince Miss Branch that she could be trusted with Valerie's secret. If she did, she reminded herself, then she could spend the rest of the week with Mark, just the two of them together with no intrusion from the problem of Valerie St John . . .

It took only seconds for her to be disillusioned. Miss Branch looked up with a cool, may-I-help-you smile as Shelby came in, but the instant she recognised her, the librarian's lips froze. 'You!' she said, with a tone of loathing.

Shelby was determined to be friendly. 'I'd like to talk to you a moment, if I may.'

'No, young lady. I'll do the talking, and you can shut up for once and listen!' Miss Branch was ignoring her own rule of quiet voices in the library, and her tone was rising. 'You and your search for this so-called writer! A publicity stunt, that's what I call it! No manners, no thought for what you're doing to other people's lives . . .'

'Miss Branch, I merely asked some people if they knew who Valerie St John might be. Your name came up——'

'Oh, yes, I heard all about it.' The librarian's eyes were fiery. 'I know about the results of your little party last night. They called me as soon as you left, and told me all about Nora's helpfulness. Smearing my reputation for no good cause, that's what you've done!'

'Miss Branch, writing a romance novel isn't something to be ashamed of——'

'You might have asked me, that's all I have to say about it!'

'I am asking you. This is the first opportunity I've had.'

'You say you're searching for someone,' the woman muttered. 'You come into town and start raising all kinds of publicity—newspaper articles and club meetings and now everyone knows all your business—— '

'I'm sorry.' Shelby was determined to placate this furious woman. 'It never occurred to me to ask you about Valerie. I quite understand that you didn't want it to become public knowledge——'

The librarian smiled grimly. 'Why, you silly girl,' she snapped. 'You think I meant that I'm Valerie—whatever her name is? Well, you're wrong! Can you understand that much? You're dead wrong!'

Shelby's first reaction was relief. *I knew that this sour woman could never write with Valerie's passion, with her understanding, with her love,* she thought.

And then Mark's cynicism popped to the surface of her mind again. *But of course she's denying it,* Shelby thought. *If Miss Branch is really Valerie, she will deny it to her dying breath, unless I can catch her in a lie.*

She put her palms flat on the glass surface of the desk and leaned forward, balancing her weight. 'Then what were you doing, Miss Branch,' she asked pleasantly, 'the day that Nora saw you sorting out an entire ream of paper into manila envelopes?'

'I'll tell you this much, Little Miss Smarty. I certainly wasn't sending out duplicate copies of some trashy love story, that's certain.'

'Oh?' Shelby refused to give up. 'What *were* you doing?'

'Why would I send duplicates, anyway?' Miss Branch asked reasonably. 'If I already have a publisher——'

'I wondered about that.' Shelby gave the woman points for thinking of that one. 'But I'm afraid, Miss Branch, that I will never believe that you aren't Valerie unless you tell me what you were so nervous about the day Nora was here. And yesterday afternoon, too, come to that. When you took Mr Buchanan and me through your office to the local history room, you were so irritable that something must have been wrong. Was I too close on your trail, Miss Branch?'

The librarian looked at her with loathing in her eyes, for a long moment. Then she turned and went back to her office, without a word. Shelby was afraid that the woman might never come back.

Then a manila envelope hit the desk in front of her. 'There it is,' Miss Branch said stiffly. 'It's a guidebook on running a small library.'

Shelby slid a fingernail under the flap and let the photocopied pages drop into her hands. 'And why did you shove it into a drawer when Nora came in that day?'

'I couldn't afford to have the book printed—it's only in the try-out stages. So I made photocopies to send around the state so other librarians can read it and tell me what needs to be added or changed.' She sounded like a child who has just tried out an idea on an idolised adult and is afraid that it will be vetoed. 'If the board finds out that I used the copy machine for that many pages they might fire me. They're very sensitive about misusing the machine——'

Shelby's eyes were on the first page. 'They won't find out from me,' she said quietly. She glanced through the booklet and put it back in the envelope.

Miss Branch said, 'Do you believe me now?' Her tone was still snappish, but no longer as angry as it had been.

Shelby nodded, and bit her lip. 'Oh, yes, I believe you,' she said finally. Valerie could never have written those long, over-complicated sentences, that flowery prose.

And I, she thought, *am right back at square one. Knowing nothing, needing to read that letter before I can do anything else—and not wanting to leave Mark here while I go back to New York . . .*

There's always the telephone, she reminded herself, and shuddered a little as she imagined how the news would flash through the whole office if Valerie's letter told her to go to hell.

Mark didn't understand that, she told herself glumly. He couldn't understand, because he'd never worked at Jonas Brothers, why she had to do it herself.

'I'm sorry to have caused you trouble, Miss Branch,' she said, quietly.

She paused at the door, automatically polite, when Miss Branch spoke. 'If you ask me,' the librarian said, a little diffidently, 'it's Patricia.'

Shelby turned around slowly; something impelled her to hear the librarian out. 'Patricia Buchanan? Why do you think that she's Valerie?'

'Because she taught English up at the college for years. She just retired last spring.'

Shelby closed her eyes in pain, and remembered a grammar book lying in the table in Pat's kitchen. *It belongs to Patty*, Mark had said. But there were lots of teachers. It didn't mean that they all wrote novels in their spare time.

'She taught all the freshman composition courses for ten years or more,' Miss Branch said. 'That's what got her involved with the library—having all her students do research here.'

It all leads back to the library. Shelby could hear her own words echoing through her head. Valerie hadn't said specifically that she was an employee of the library; she could have meant that she was a volunteer. And Pat was not only a volunteer, but a member of the library's board of trustees . . .

'It's been staring me in the face all week,' Shelby muttered, and slapped her hand down hard on the desktop. It stung, but she didn't even notice. 'Why didn't you tell me this earlier?' she accused.

'Because you never asked,' Miss Branch said simply. 'Besides, I just confirmed it myself this morning.' She half-smiled. 'Call it self-protection, if you will, but I didn't get very curious until after the finger was pointed at me.'

'There's proof that Patricia Buchanan is Valerie?' Shelby asked eagerly.

'I don't know about proof, but—here, judge it for yourself.' She took a leather-bound volume from under the counter.

'The Buchanan family history,' Shelby said. 'What about it?'

'No,' Miss Branch corrected. 'The Warren family history. Pat's mother was a Warren, and Pat would be the first to tell you that the Buchanans are merely incidental—a two-generation newcomer to the line. The important one, to her, is the Warren family.'

Shelby remembered what Mark had said about the Buchanans being upstarts, and smiled. 'I know that the Warren family line dates hundreds of years back, to Europe,' she said.

Miss Branch nodded. 'You must have read the first chapter or two of her book.'

'Something like that,' Shelby conceded, and could have kicked herself for not picking up the book earlier. She had had a dozen chances, including once in the local history room, when Mark had almost taken it out of her hands.

She started to laugh. She couldn't wait to tell Mark. When he found out how close they had been to Valerie all week, he would start to scream about wasted time——

But Mark already knew. Mark must have known.

The knowledge hit Shelby with the impact of a ten-ton truck. Mark had said himself this morning that he was closer to Pat than to any other member of his family. It was unlikely that she would have kept such a secret from him. And after all, he was living in Pat's house—it would be almost impossible for Pat to have kept the knowledge from him.

She thought about the last few days, and realised that Mark had spent the week covering up for Pat, deliberately keeping her secret—feeding Shelby false clues and leading her down false trails. Yes, Mark knew Valerie St John intimately. It had been no accident that he had told Shelby not to waste her time on Pat's book; he had been afraid that Shelby would recognise Valerie's style, as she had once bragged that she could . . .

Miss Branch had been chattering on about her search and her discovery. 'Here it is,' she said, and turned the book around to face Shelby. 'That family pedigree is one of the most important things in Patricia's life,' she said. 'The Warrens were distinguished people in Europe. Then one of the younger sons got an itch to try the New World. He was the first Warren to come to America, and his name was——' Her finger traced down the diagram and stopped.

Shelby's voice was hoarse as she read the bold black type. 'Edward St John Warren? I don't believe it!'

'It's just the kind of thing Patricia would do, though.'

Shelby nodded slowly. 'That ties it up,' she said faintly.

Mark, she was thinking. *Why, my love, did you lie to me?*

CHAPTER ELEVEN

SHE stumbled back toward Patricia Buchanan's house, sick at heart. *How dumb can you be?* she accused herself. She'd had a known author—self-published, to be sure, but one of the few people in this town who can point to a real, honest-to-goodness book between two hard covers, and not just a manuscript or an idea that someday might be a novel. A real published author— and she'd been stupid enough to ignore her because she'd paid the publishing bill herself, and because no one had pointed a finger at Patricia. Had they all known? she wondered. Had the whole thing been a conspiracy?

'Dumb,' she said. 'Shelby, you're a dumb blonde.'

She had suspected everyone else who suggested a candidate, but she had accepted Pat's list of possibilities—transmitted through Mark—at face value and ignored the possibility that it was a false clue. She had looked at the rows of packed shelves in Pat's living-room and forgotten that Valerie collected books. She had accepted Mark's word that Valerie's post-office box had no other name listed—and Mark's word, like Pat's, was worth nothing . . .

She was frantically anxious to talk to Mark, to confront him with the truth and to demand an explanation of his behaviour. 'If there can be any explanation that makes sense,' she confessed under her breath.

What reason could Mark give for purposely keeping her in the dark? Had he promised his co-operation to Pat, and then been unable to back out? Had he regretted, as he got to know Shelby better, the fact that he had become involved in the deception? In the last day, he had seemed impatient to be rid of Valerie. He'd even called her a 'blasted nuisance'. Had he been wishing that things had been honest between them—that he could confess the truth?

Or had he enjoyed the whole thing? Shelby remembered all the jokes he had made about Valerie's name, and his ever-present suggestions for a new place to look. He'd even insisted, in a nice way, that she must read all of those awful manuscripts, by telling her that Valerie might have slipped something into the pile. And all the time he had known perfectly well that Valerie was out of town . . .

How he must have been laughing at her behind her back, Shelby thought, and fury boiled along her veins. So he thought it was so damned funny, did he?

Well, Mr Mark Buchanan, she thought, *I figured it all out, no thanks to you. And now you're going to listen to what I have to say about it in a few minutes!*

She climbed the hill towards Pat's house faster than ever before, driven on by her anger and the nagging ache in the pit of her stomach that begged to know why he had done this to her. And she remembered, as she neared the gleaming white house, that Mark had ignored her that first day. He had told her that he was unwilling to help find yet another hack writer, that he had too many important things to do. And yet that very night when he had appeared at her door with a changed attitude, she had been so grateful to see him that she had not questioned his motives.

Now, she thought bitterly, she could see the whole thing. He had talked to Lora that afternoon and gathered the details; he must have then called Pat and warned her, and given her his promise to keep Shelby off her trail. No wonder Patricia had not come storming home to check up on Mark's behaviour!

'We'll see about that, Miss Valerie St John,' Shelby

muttered under her breath. 'We'll just see about that.' After she'd settled something with Mark, she amended.

And her heart ached even more. *How could he lie to me?* she screamed inside. *Did he hold me, and kiss me, and make love to me, just to keep me occupied and off balance, so that I wouldn't find Valerie?*

If that was his motive he has certainly succeeded, she thought bitterly. She'd been willing to forget the world, if she could have Mark. And he knew it—and he used that knowledge against her.

The ladders were propped against the side of the house, but Mark was nowhere to be seen. Had he suspected this morning that his time was running out, that the delaying manoeuvres were no longer effective? Or was he inside the house, innocently drinking coffee and waiting for her to come back so that they could start painting together?

I'll show him paint, Shelby thought grimly. *It's lucky for him that he isn't out here where there's a gallon I could throw at him . . .*

She climbed the steps to the front door, half-hoping that he would be there, half-wishing that he was not. Now that it was too late to gather her thoughts, she realized that she didn't really know what she wanted to say to him. How could she make him understand the pain she was suffering because of his lies?

She couldn't stand to tell him everything. She didn't want him to know how badly she hurt, because then he would know how much she had cared about him. If she hadn't loved him so, Shelby thought, then this falsehood that he had lived all week wouldn't matter.

But once he knew how much she loved him then he might use that against her too.

He was capable of that, she knew. He was quite able to twist her heart with his charm, with his smile. And he would do it, Shelby knew, if it would benefit him, or Pat.

Desolation settled like a blank, cold mist into her bones. All she had wanted was to talk to Valerie, and Mark had known that. Even if Patricia had been wary, Mark at least should have known that he could have trusted her.

I must be very careful, she thought, *or I will be used again.*

There was no sound in the house. She tiptoed across the living-room, listening intently, not even knowing what she hoped to hear. If Mark were there, at least it would be over soon, all the nasty words said and the recriminations past. What happened after that, she didn't know—and at this moment Shelby didn't care.

But if he wasn't there then she would have to wait. It would be hard on her, but it would also give her time to gather the facts that would make it impossible for Mark to deny the truth any longer. She picked up the family history volume from the coffee-table. Had he seen it lying there? she wondered. Had he known what she would find hidden there?

It would take some solid facts to break down his denial. He had done it so well, with such dramatic effects, for four days, that Shelby could not imagine him easily admitting to the truth now. She would have to prove to him that she knew.

Still there was no sound in the house. She checked each downstairs room, putting her head in just long enough to be certain that Mark wasn't there. Finally, in the kitchen, she found a note.

'Went to the hardware store for more paint. Back in half an hour,' it said.

Not a word of greeting, regret, caring—'What did you expect, Shelby?' she asked herself crossly. 'He's not likely to sign himself "Love, Mark" after the squabble you had with him this morning.'

It left her feeling even more hurt. He'd mentioned the possibility of Shelby spending the winter with him in

Florida, but apparently that idea had quickly passed. He hadn't even waited around to talk to her, to try to sort out this disagreement.

Yet at the same time, she felt an irrational sense of relief that he was gone. At last she would not have to face him right away; it would give her a little time to gather her thoughts, to decide what she wanted to say to him.

She picked the note up and read it again, then shoved it into the pocket of her jacket. He had left the small slip of paper atop a folded pair of jeans and a pullover shirt. Mark was apparently expecting her to be on a ladder when he got back.

'He's going to get several surprises,' Shelby muttered. Her jaw set determinedly as she thought about the house. Where was she most likely to find evidence that Patricia Buchanan was indeed Valerie?

The spare bedroom upstairs, she decided. She'd never seen the other rooms; only the door of Mark's room—the guest room—had been left open. But the extra bedroom was the most likely place for a home office to be located. Valerie must keep her typewriter somewhere, and that was probably it.

She felt like a cat burglar as she climbed the stairs. One squeaked under her weight, and Shelby jumped and almost cried out. 'Silly,' she lectured herself, 'it's not as though you're doing anything illegal.' Unethical, perhaps—snooping was not part of Shelby's code of honour. But certainly Mark and Pat had asked for this.

She found herself in Patricia's bedroom. It was pale blue, with a ruffled canopy above the bed and a matching skirted dressing table. 'Somehow I expected pink,' Shelby said under her breath. She glanced around, but could see nothing suspicious. Unless Patricia/Valerie hid her manuscripts under the bed, the room was innocent.

The extra bedroom between Patricia's and the guest

room, was small. Shelby stood in the doorway and sucked in a deep breath. She had struck paydirt.

It was an office, as compact and efficient a one as Shelby had ever seen. The windows were covered by neat narrow blinds. A businesslike desk was in the centre of the room, and the walls were lined with shelves, with books spilling over on to the floor. A typewriter stood uncovered on a stand near the desk; Shelby glanced at the model and nodded. Valerie's manuscripts had been typed on that brand of machine. It was one of the more expensive typewriters on the market. Valerie always had the best of everything, she reflected.

The desk top was clear except for an appointment book and a desk blotter on which cryptic notes were jotted. To one side lay a single book—a picture book of African art. It was all the confirmation Shelby needed. 'A methodical girl, our Valerie,' she told herself. 'I wonder where she did her research for the love scenes?' She was trying to joke away the pain. The attempt nearly choked her. She could no longer feel the anticipation of at last meeting Valerie. For Valerie had run from her, dodged her, lied to avoid her, schemed to deceive her . . .

I want to know why, she thought bitterly. *Why was she so unwilling to talk to me? After all those months, the dozens of letters, the friendship we had built together——* *It was friendship,* Shelby told herself. *I know it was, because even though Valerie never told me much about herself, she shared a few important things. And she cared about me, too. She really cared.* That wasn't imaginary; it wasn't put on. It was real.

So if Valerie cared so much, why wouldn't Patricia talk to her now? *I will know,* she swore to herself. *If I have to, I will make another trip out here to get the answers that I need to hear.*

I'll come back to Warren's Grove, she added

sombrely, *after I'm certain that Mark is safely in Florida for the winter.*

But this fretting wasn't gathering the evidence she needed to show Mark that she knew what she was talking about. She hesitated, and then she sat down in the big, comfortable chair and started to look tentatively through Patricia's desk drawers.

'I feel as if I'm intruding on sacred ground,' she said softly. It sounded a little silly out loud, and she forced herself to smile and keep looking.

The bottom drawer of the desk was locked, and Shelby bit her lip and sat there quietly for a moment, considering. She was no safecracker, and she had no wish to damage Patricia's desk. But whatever was in that drawer must be vitally important to her case.

Keys, she thought. There must be a key here somewhere; it was unlikely that Pat would run to get her handbag every time she needed to open her bottom drawer.

Or had she simply locked it before she left the house in Mark's care, to prevent him from doing the very thing that Shelby was now doing? In that case, she considered, was it possible that Mark might not know the truth? Could he have been perfectly honest with her after all?

Her heart made a sudden, glad leap. Perhaps it was all possible after all. Mark would be as glad as she to have the mystery solved—

After all, she thought, he had begged her this morning to stay a few days longer so that she could meet Pat. Surely a conspirator would not have encouraged her to stay in Warren's Grove. And he had not hidden Pat's book; he had even told her yesterday, when they were at the library, that there was a copy at the house. Those things indicated that he had not been suspicious. And if Mark was indeed innocent—— It changed everything, Shelby thought, and her heart began to pound in quickstep. She had to find out for sure, she told herself.

She opened the top drawer again, and, moved by sheer caprice, lifted out the divider tray that held Pat's rubber bands and paper clips and tacks. And there, nestled in the bottom of the drawer, lay a tiny silver key.

Shelby snatched it up and inserted it in the lock. It slid and turned in one smooth, silent motion, and the lock vibrated open under her hand.

She sat there for a long moment, afraid of what she might find. Then she swallowed hard and pulled the drawer out.

Right on top was a stationery box. Shelby picked it up, only half aware of what she was doing, and opened it. The scent of lilacs rose in a wave from the paper and assaulted her nose. 'Valerie,' she murmured, and for the first time she really believed the evidence of her own eyes. This was solid. This was proof.

A tiny box was stuffed with heart-shaped address labels bearing Valerie's name and the post-office box number. And underneath the stationery was a row of paperback books.

'Valerie's own copies,' Shelby said, remembering the day when she had put that first small book into an envelope and addressed it, knowing that it would soon be bringing delight and pride to the author.

And suddenly Shelby knew why she was so upset at the idea that Valerie wanted nothing to do with her. 'I feel betrayed,' she exclaimed. 'I worked hard for her—I tried so hard to make her care about me. And now that I ask her to help me, she refuses to even listen to my problem.'

She picked up the copy of Valerie's first book. It had collected the scent of violets from being closed in the drawer with the stationery. 'This is not a mint copy,' she mused. 'It's been read at least once.'

She turned to the opening page, willing herself again to feel the thrill of that first reading. But her eye was caught instead by the title page and by Valerie's angular signature inscribed across it.

She held it up, and suddenly her whole body was so tense that she couldn't get air into her lungs. For the signature was not the familiar 'Valerie St John' that ended the letters in the file back in Shelby's hotel room.

This book was signed, 'Valerie Minneapolis-St Paul.'

She stared at it for a long moment, and then she tossed it aside and reached for another copy. One was signed 'Valerie St Peter's Basilica.' Another was 'Valerie San Juan, Puerto Rico.' The autograph on the last book read 'Valerie St Croix, Virgin Islands.'

Shelby looked down at the books, and almost unwilling, her hand went to her jacket pocket. 'I've seen that writing before,' she murmured, and pulled out the note that she had found on the kitchen table.

And then she knew. Valerie wasn't Patricia Buchanan at all. It had not been Pat who had signed Valerie's name to those books. And to the letters. And to the contracts locked safely away in her office in New York City . . .

Mark was Valerie St John.

Shelby didn't know how long she sat there, in shock, horrified by her discovery. Then, abruptly, a door banged under the office window, and she jumped out of her chair. 'I can't face him,' she said, feeling a little hysterical. 'I can't!'

She looked out the window and saw that the neighbours were just getting into their car. She felt like sagging against the wall, but she pulled herself together, flung the books back into the drawer, locked it, and replaced the key. She had to get out of Patricia's house before Mark came back.

It had been bad enough, she thought bitterly, when she thought that he had lied to protect his aunt. But Mark had certainly known how important it was to her to find Valerie. And he had lied to her, misled her, tantalised her, made fun of her——

Made love to her, simply to keep her from pursuing the search for Valerie.

Shelby bit her lip till it bled. That she could never forgive, she vowed. She had to get out of Warren's Grove. She could not look at Mark right now, knowing what he had done. She could not bear to listen to explanations that could never convince her. She could not endure being subjected to that consummate charm, and she knew that he would use it if given the opportunity . . .

She pulled the front door shut behind her and stood a moment on the steps, uncertain. Which way was the hardware store? she wondered. Would he be coming up the hill or down, when he returned? How could she best get back to the hotel without being seen?

In the end it made no difference. She caught not a glimpse of his moss-green sports car. Perhaps, she thought as she threw her clothes haphazardly into her bags, he couldn't bring himself to face her, and he was staying away till he knew she had gone.

Just as well, she thought savagely. There was no excuse for what Mark had done, and if he tried to explain it, she would probably bury her fingernails in his handsome face and rip it to shreds. This way at least she had a little dignity left, as well as the knowledge that, foolish as she had been, she had at least got out before she had completely destroyed herself.

When her bags were packed, she made one last quick inspection of the room to be sure that she had left nothing behind. The silk daffodil that he had brought her on that first night lay on the night table, and Shelby picked it up and cradled it, half-consciously, against her cheek.

'You fool,' she told herself, 'sentimental fool.' She picked up her bags, folded her jacket across her arm, and carried everything down the stairs. She would shred the daffodil and leave it for him at the desk with her compliments. That should relieve any doubts he had about her state of mind.

The manager looked stunned. 'You're leaving us already?' she stammered.

'Yes. I have to make the train—do I have time?' Shelby asked. She was briskly signing her name to travellers' cheques and hoping that the manager wouldn't ask too many questions.

'You have about fifteen minutes. You've pushed it rather close, Miss Stuart, but I'll get the bellboy to help you up to the station.'

'Thanks.' Shelby forced a smile, but she felt as if it was glued on to her face. 'I appreciate everything you've done for me.'

Including, she thought, *the night that you kept me from giving in to Mark. It wasn't your fault that I couldn't continue to resist that invincible charm . . .*

'I hope it's nothing we've done,' the manager sounded puzzled and upset.

'Oh, no! I've been called back to New York earlier than I expected.'

'And what about Valerie St John?' the woman asked curiously.

Valerie, Shelby heart cried. *My love, my love——*

'Valerie doesn't matter any more,' she said steadily.

The train ride was long and tedious. Even though she had thought the trip from Chicago to Warren's Grove was endless, it had at least been relieved by optimistic hope for the future. Now there was only endless black, and the knowledge that Mark's treachery had robbed her of any chance to protect her job.

'Some saint,' she muttered. 'Valerie turned out to be a Judas instead.'

Now that the first shock was wearing off, she was beginning to be angry with herself. How could she have been so foolish? Mark had known things that he should not have known—she could see that now. For someone who said he had never read a romance novel, he had known a great deal about the form. For an author who had never dealt with Jonas Brothers, he knew a lot about the firm. And Shelby had never noticed.

She had never seriously considered the possibility of a man. Mark himself had laughed off the notion when she had pulled the deputy sheriff's name off the book cards at the library. And yet all the signs had been there.

Valerie liked to play with words, and Mark had toyed with puns and semantics all week. Valerie hated elaborate food, and Mark had discussed, over endless steaks and cheeseburgers, his lack of knowledge of gourmet cooking. Valerie had a wide knowledge of men, and when Shelby had mentioned that, Mark had nearly fallen out of his chair laughing——

Shelby's cheeks burned. 'You're a damn' fool,' she accused herself. 'A damned, stupid fool.'

In Chicago she shared a cab from the downtown train station to O'Hare Airport, and was viciously rude to the businessman who paid half the fare and tried to engage in a mild flirtation on the way. The only seat available was a first-class one on a champagne flight; it was that or wait till the next morning for the regular rates. Shelby didn't even hesitate before she handed over her credit card. She'd worry next month about how to pay it back, she decided. Right now she just wanted to get home as soon as possible.

She checked her bags and looked for a telephone booth so she could give Lora her flight number. Lora's new secretary answered her phone, and Shelby had a time convincing her that she was not a crackpot, but finally Lora picked up the extension. 'What's the matter, Shelby?' she asked. 'Are the Indians chasing you back to civilization?'

'Just pick me up at Kennedy, Lora.'

'Are you bringing Valerie's scalp back with you?' Her tone was polite, vaguely interested. Shelby wondered if Lora knew what her precious client was doing, or if he had engaged in a new career behind his agent's back. *If Lora knows*, she decided, *and she let me get into this without telling me, I'll kill her. No questions asked, no mercy.*

The champagne was a good vintage, and Shelby didn't turn it down. *I don't care what happens to me*, she thought, and pushed aside the thought that there would be no Mark, and no miracle cure, if she had a hangover in the morning.

She didn't care about much of anything right now, she told herself, and reached into her tote bag for a tissue to dry the moisture that seemed to collect in the corners of her eyes. The silk daffodil peeked out of the side pocket of the bag. She had forgotten to leave it at the hotel, she realised.

He deserved a lot worse than his flower back, she thought viciously. He deserved to be blacklisted. She could tell Lora what he'd done. She could tell her friends at his publishing company, she could——

But she would do none of it, she knew. She blew her nose defiantly, and then wrapped the daffodil carefully in a cocktail napkin and put it away safely. She would not seek to harm him. She loved him too much to hurt him, no matter how much he had hurt her. Instead of plotting revenge, she asked the flight attendant for another glass of champagne.

Loara was waiting at the gate, her mink jacket carelessly tossed over her shoulders. By that time the champagne had dulled the ache in Shelby's heart, and she was able to smile as she came down the ramp.

'You're sloshed,' Lora accused, after one look at her friend.

Shelby smiled. 'In a week of disasters,' she announced, enunciating carefully, 'something finally went right. I do love champagne flights, Lora.'

'It certainly looks that way,' Lora said. 'How was your trip, now that you mention it?'

Shelby stopped in the middle of the terminal to consider it. Then she smiled broadly and announced, 'Lora, it was positively—saintly!'

And then the tears began to flow.

CHAPTER TWELVE

SHELBY finished reading the last page, and set the manuscript aside with a contented sigh. Maria Martin's new book was her best yet—warm, sexy, utterly satisfying and powerful. Shelby turned her chair towards the window and sipped her coffee, thinking about what she should tell Maria about this new work.

A golden October lay across Manhattan. It was cool down on the streets, where the caverns formed by the skyscrapers seldom caught the sun, but from Shelby's window the city looked its best on an afternoon in late autumn. Soon the leaves would fall and winter would descend in strict black and white.

It had been a month since she had left Warren's Grove, fleeing from Mark as if a pack of bloodhounds was at her heels. 'Silly,' she told herself now, in the peacefulness of a quiet day at the office. She should have stayed and confronted him, told him calmly that she had untangled his little secret. What difference did it make to Shelby, anyway—what Mark said, what he did? It had been but a summer romance—a brief affair that she had foolishly mistaken for love.

Instead, she had run back to New York, like a teenager who has suddenly discovered that her charming prince has a flaw, and now she regretted that they had not come to some kind of truth between them and avoided this embarrassing silence.

For in the last month, the only communication she had received was the letter from Valerie which had been waiting on her desk for her return. Shelby set her cup down and searched out the folder in her desk drawer to refresh her memory. Already, she thought wearily, it seems so long ago. So much like a dream . . . not reality at all.

'I can't stand it,' Valerie had written. 'It's been three weeks since I swore off writing romances, and I'm going crazy. Expect my new book soon—this one may actually write itself.' And the signature had been the angular, spiky 'Valerie St John' that Shelby had come to know over the years.

She didn't know if she was still to expect the new book; the letter had been postmarked the day after she had arrived in Warren's Grove. Mark had known that she was in town, and that she was looking for Valerie, when he had sent the letter. But since it had been posted, a lot of things had changed, and Shelby didn't know if Mark had actually intended to write a new book or if the letter had been just another ploy to convince her to give up the search.

No wonder he had been so anxious for her to know what was in that letter, she thought. If she had asked the secretary to read it, that day when she had called the office, she would instantly have stopped looking for Valerie. That was what Mark had wanted. It was probably all that he had wanted, she reflected morosely.

At any rate, whether Valerie St John produced a new book or not didn't really matter now. Shelby's job was safe, for at least as long as it took to find a better one. Maria Martin's new manuscript was a sure-fire seller, and the letter from Valerie was evidence enough of her intentions. It should even convince Bob Jonas, if he started asking questions. After all, Shelby could tell him if the new book didn't come in, even excellent writers hit dry spells now and then.

Shelby hadn't answered Valerie's letter. There had seemed to be nothing more to say. What could she write to a person she had thought she loved—a man who had deceived her, lied to her, used her?

'It's over now,' she told herself. 'I paid a price to find Valerie, and now I'm free.'

But Shelby couldn't see the sadness that had settled around her eyes, and the tightness of her mouth, and the hollows in her cheeks.

She wrote a short, cheerful note to Maria, telling her how wonderful the new book was. Then she poured herself another cup of coffee and picked up the next manuscript.

Lora called at midafternoon. 'I haven't talked to you in weeks,' she reminded. 'Which, translated, means that you haven't called me. What's wrong, Shelby? Are you ready to talk about it?'

'About what, Lora?'

'You know perfectly well what I'm referring to. It isn't like you to get off a plane so inebriated that you can hardly stand up, and then have hysterics in the terminal.'

'I don't plan to make a habit of it, Lora, so let's let it drop, all right?'

Lora sighed. 'If you would talk about whatever happened out there—— Are you coming to my cocktail party tonight?'

'Not if you intend to cross-examine me, no.'

'I promise,' Lora said hastily, 'I won't even speak to you unless you say something first. Is that good enough?'

'I'll think about it.'

'You'd better come. In the first place, it's time to stop hiding in your office and get out among people again. And besides, there will be a couple of job possibilities running around tonight. Are you still planning to leave Jonas Brothers?'

Shelby's fingertip unconsciously caressed the silk daffodil in the crystal vase on her desktop. 'Yes, I'm still looking. It's time for me to move on.'

And when Valerie's next book comes in, she thought, *I won't be here to read it . . .*

'Get dolled up, and come prepared to impress them with your qualifications,' Lora recommended. 'See you tonight.'

Shelby sat for a long time, staring down at the pink envelope that Valerie's last letter had come in. The lilac scent was vague now, like an antique sachet. If Mark cared about her, she thought, if he cared even the least little bit, he would have called by now, or he would have written. But there had been nothing.

She wished he had called. She would have liked to give the secretary a message—*Tell him I'm in conference and I'll be available next year. Tell him I died and left no forwarding address* . . .

But there had been no opportunity for such sarcasm. It was all over, and she had meant so little to him that he hadn't even bothered to make a formal end to the affair.

She straightened her shoulders defiantly. She would go to Lora's party tonight, and she would set herself whole-heartedly to impress the people who had jobs to offer. With Lora's help she could get one of those jobs, she was certain of it.

But she couldn't keep her fingers from reaching out to the silk daffodil. She touched it gently, almost apologetically, as if she were saying goodbye.

Lora was wearing deep green tonight, something long, flowing, and backless which made her eyes look like the Atlantic Ocean. When Shelby arrived the cocktail party was already loud, and Lora was enthusiastically hugging a tall, white-haired man. She finally let him go and turned to see Shelby in the doorway.

'Nice,' she said, her gaze flicking over Shelby's blue velvet jacket and muted plaid skirt. 'Professional, and yet feminine . . .' Her eyes met Shelby's. 'Mark Buchanan is here tonight,' she said bluntly.

Shelby was absolutely still for a few seconds. Then

she shrugged. 'I'd rather not stay, then. I'll see you some other time, Lora.'

Lora's voice caught her as she turned to leave. 'If you go, Shelby,' she said, very clearly, 'I will tell him that you ran away. A childish thing to do, I'd say—dodging him like that.'

Shelby said, over her shoulder, 'Don't you think that's my business?'

'I'm concerned for you, Shelby. You're ten pounds lighter, and you never smile any more. Something happened to you out in that godforsaken wilderness, and I finally know what it was. I just want to help you——'

'So Mark told you what happened?'

'No,' Lora said quietly, 'you just did, when you chose to leave rather than face him. He hasn't said a word to me about it.'

'How kind of you to be concerned.' Shelby's voice was cutting.

'It's not entirely altruistic, I'll admit,' Lora said. 'He hasn't written a word for me in more than a month, and frankly I'm getting a little worried.'

'I'd suggest you ask him to explain that,' Shelby suggested sweetly. 'I'm sure he'll have a convincing story—he always does!' She turned from Lora and tried to lose herself in the crowd. The delay had done one thing; she had concluded that she would not give up her best chance at a new job just because Mark was present. Damn Mark anyway; she'd show him just how little he meant to her!

She glanced around the room, but nowhere could she see a tall man with perpetually rumpled dark hair. Perhaps, she thought, he's off in one of Lora's secluded corners with the prettiest of the female guests . . . She hope that he didn't hide away all evening. It would be best for both of them to get this matter settled, once and for all.

Rodney was standing beside the bar when Shelby asked the bartender for a ginger ale.

'How was your vacation?' he asked, draining his glass and pushing it across the bar for a refill.

'Entertaining.' As she had intended, the word was crisp and meaningless. She wondered what Rodney would have said if she had told him that she'd spent the week having a flaming affair with Valerie St John. It would almost be worth the uproar, just to watch his face.

He grunted. 'I understand you're looking for a job. We might have an opening for a good editor, especially one who already had some valuable contacts with established writers.'

Shelby put one elbow on the padded rail of the bar and leaned on it. She looked up at him steadily for a long moment, sipped her ginger ale, and then countered his question with one of her own. 'Who's your source inside Jonas Brothers?'

Rodney raised an eyebrow. 'Who says I have one?'

'Elementary deduction.'

'Tell you what, Shelby, have dinner with me after the party and I'll tell you. In return for a few bits of information from you, of course.'

Including Valerie St John's phone number, Shelby thought. She was tempted to give it to him. It should be an unforgettable experience for everyone.

'Terribly sorry to disappoint you,' said a voice from over Shelby's shoulder, and cold chills chased each other up and down her spine, 'but Shelby will be busy after the party.'

She didn't even look up. She could have closed her eyes and still painted Mark from memory as he stood there, because she knew his expression so well. There would be no hint of humour in his dark eyes right now, just as there was no trace of uncertainty in his voice.

All right, she told herself. *You wanted to get this straightened out. Now is your chance.*

She forced herself to turn her head, but she avoided Mark's eyes. She didn't want to see what emotion lay in the dark depths. And she thought, sadly, that it was one thing to think that she wanted to see him, to talk to him, to get everything out in the open—but it was quite another thing actually to do it.

'I'm sure that we can be finished with our little chat well before Rodney is ready to go to dinner, Mark,' she said, keeping her voice steady with an effort.

'I'm afraid not, Shelby.' His voice was just as level, but a threat hovered just under the surface. Shelby saw his eyes flick over Rodney's face, and interpreted the tiny lift of his eyebrow as astonishment. 'Say goodnight to the gentleman now.'

It was patently an order, just the kind of attitude that Shelby would ordinarily have crushed with icy, calculated rudeness. But she sensed, from the expression on Rodney's face, that dinner with him tonight would be an inquisition. She wasn't in the mood to play question games with Rodney, but neither was she in the mood to be ordered around by Mark Buchanan——

She looked up, intending to tell him just that. His eyes looked almost black, and there was something there that took hold of her heart and shook it. He was pleading with her, silently—he was begging.

Shelby drew a long, shuddering breath, and in that instant she knew how foolish she had been. In the last few weeks without him, she had convinced herself that it hadn't mattered after all, that it had been only a summer romance that—like all her other infatuations— would blow over, given time and absence.

Now she knew better. One glimpse of that flash of humility in his eyes, and she was lost. *I love him*, she thought. *I will always love him, no matter what he did to me.*

'I thought you hated New York,' she whispered. She knew that it sounded inane.

'I do,' he said. 'But sometimes pressing business leaves me no alternative but to come here.'

'And what is that pressing business? Talking to Lora about your next book?'

'Sometimes,' he said, 'I can only find what I need in the city.'

Rodney shook his head as if to clear it. 'Do you two realise that you sound like a bad movie?' he asked.

Mark flashed a smile. It was not a pleasant one. 'Why don't you take yourself away, then?' he asked.

'Because I'm next to the bar,' Rodney said sweetly, 'and I plan to stay here.'

Mark ignored him. 'Come with me, Shelby?'

Her hands were clenched so tightly on the stem of her glass that her knuckles were white. She nodded, feeling like a little child who had strayed out into a world full of fog. The room was quiet now, she noticed—or was it just that her ears had tuned out the noise? No one else seemed to notice anything strange.

He led her back along a hallway and opened a door. Shelby stopped on the threshhold and looked around. She'd never been in Lora's bedroom before, but it was obvious that Mark had. He hadn't even hesitated, and he didn't look startled at the surroundings.

The room looked like a Hollywodd remake of *The Arabian Nights*. Everything Lora owned was elegant and expensive, but she had really let herself go here. Everything was silver, from the curtains, which looked like spun threads of gleaming metal, to the tiny telephone on the night-table. The bed was round, draped with silvery lace, and the canopy above it was caught back with wide bows in silver satin. The whole thing was a boudoir for a princess, and it left Shelby feeling very much like the frog.

Why had he brought her here? she wondered. Did he intend to show her just how much difference there was between them?

Shelby walked across the room and sat down on the upholstered bench in front of Lora's dressing table. 'You certainly know your way around Lora's apartment.'

'I stay here often when I'm in New York.'

It answered several questions. She had suspected as much, after all, but the pain of knowing was almost more than she could bear. Shelby let the silence drag on for a long moment, and then said, 'I thought you wanted to talk to me, or shall I go back to the party?'

'Are you all right, Shelby?' His voice was diffident, hesitant. 'You look as though you've been ill.'

'Quite all right.' She was irritated that he had even asked. It was just another way of manipulating her— making her feel as if he really cared. 'And how is your intimate friend Valerie St Mark?' she asked sweetly.

He bit his lip, and sighed. 'Is that why you left Warren's Grove?'

'Give the man a gold medal for his prize!' she jibed. 'Did you think I left because I'd turn into a pumpkin if I didn't get home by midnight?'

'I'm sorry about Valerie, Shelby.' He sat down on the edge of Lora's bed.

'Sorry?' she whispered unbelievingly. 'You're sorry? Well, isn't that big of you!' She gave in to the rage that was growing in the pit of her stomach. 'You used me, and laughed at me, and lied to me, and now you say you're sorry and that's supposed to make it all right again?' She jumped up and paced across the room, needing to work off her agitation. 'What happened, Mark? Was I just a little too smart after all? I didn't feel very smart, believe me!'

'No! Shelby, listen to me, please. I never lied to you, sweetheart, I swear——'

She turned on him. 'Don't call me that,' she spat. 'You have no right!' For a moment they were face to face, staring at each other with only inches between them. Shelby backed away then, and sat down again on the dressing bench, huddling there as if she were freezing.

'I never lied to you,' he repeated softly. 'I might not have always volunteered the whole truth, but I never lied.'

'Interesting code of ethics, that,' Shelby said. She lifted her chin defiantly. 'What about all the nasty remarks about Valerie's writing style?'

'I didn't take that fluff seriously, that was sure. Half the fun of writing it was the clichés——' There was a long pause. 'Shel, you took me by surprise,' he said. 'I didn't have any idea you were looking for Valerie until you turned up at the bottom of my ladder that morning. The whole town of Warren's Grove to choose from, and you came straight to me as if you'd been drawn there.'

'Blame your friend Lora for that,' she said sulkily.

'All I did, Shelby, was to defend myself the only way I knew how—by playing dumb about Valerie.'

Shelby toyed with the monogrammed silver top of a crystal perfume bottle.

'Think about it, Shelby,' he went on, a whimsical note in his voice. 'If it had been you, would you have come swarming down the ladder and said, "Yes, I'm Valerie, and won't you tell me why you're looking for me?" Be realistic, dear heart.'

She rearranged the bottles into a geometric pattern. He was right about that much, she had to admit. Of course he had been suspicious of her motives. But then why had he searched her out and pretended to help her?

'Grant me the right to have a few doubts, too,' he said softly. He had crossed the room, silent-footed, and was standing behind her, one hand extended as if he feared to touch her. 'You said once that you were afraid to meet Valerie because she might not be what you wanted her to be,' he reminded.

'I remember.' Shelby's voice was dry.

'I felt the same fear. All that I knew about Shelby Stuart was what she'd written to me, and letters don't tell everything.'

'You should know,' Shelby muttered, 'you're the expert when it comes to letters that say nothing.'

He winced a little, and then went on. 'I didn't have any way of knowing then, if the real girl inside was as honest and as trustworthy—and as lovely—as I wanted her to be.'

'So you lied to me.' He made a gesture of denial, and Shelby waved it away. 'All right, I believe that you told the literal truth—but you lived a lie, Mark. Why did you even come and see me? Why couldn't you just leave me alone?'

'I couldn't stay away,' he said. 'I thought about you all that afternoon—how tiny you were, and how proud, and how beautiful—and I had to find out which you really were—the shrew who'd stood under that ladder and yelled at me, or the lovely woman who wrote me those letters.'

She moved all Lora's silver bottles into a new pattern. 'So you went on helping me look for Valerie, when all the time you were keeping me away——'

'I was stuck, Shelby. All it took was that first night's dinner, and I knew that you were everything I wanted you to be. But then it was too late. I couldn't come back to you and say, "Look, I just remembered something—I'm Valerie St John." And the longer I waited, looking for an opportunity to tell you the truth, the worse it got. I kept falling deeper and deeper . . .'

'In trouble,' Shelby finished for him. She wouldn't look at him. She didn't want to see the expression in his eyes, for she didn't know if she could trust it to be the truth.

'Not quite,' he said, very softly. His hand brushed her hair. 'I was falling in love, Shelby.'

She looked up then, astonished, and found in his face

had a whole sackful of romances that someone had donated to the library, and in desperation I read them. It was something to do——'

'And you declared that you could do something just as good,' Shelby added.

She knew that he was smiling. 'Aunt Pat got tired of me bellowing about it, and she finally told me to either prove it or shut up.'

'It must have wounded your writer's pride.'

'That's right. I never intended to submit the darn thing—that wasn't in the bet—but Pat kept after me till I sent it in just to get her to quit nagging.'

'And I accepted it with glee.' Shelby remembered the day that she had finished reading that first manuscript.

'I never dreamed that it would get serious, Shel. I never even told Lora what I was doing.'

'Isn't that a little shady—not telling your agent?'

'No. We don't have an exclusive arrangement—she doesn't handle everything I write. This was between Valerie and her editor.'

He released her suddenly and Shelby, bereft of the support of his strength, nearly fell over. He opened a drawer in the small table beside Lora's bed and handed Shelby a manila envelope. 'The new book,' he said.

But I don't want a new book, she was screaming inside. *Can't you see, Mark? I want you!*

She tried to keep her voice casual. 'And you keep it in Lora's night-table? Are you certain you don't sleep here?' she asked, turning the envelope in her hand.

'Positive. I'd have taken you to the guest room except that it's full of coats and women giggling over their clothing adjustment.' His eyes gleamed.

'I'll read it tomorrow,' she promised.

'Will you do it tonight, Shel? It isn't finished, you know—I need some help on the fine points.'

She was disappointed, but she tried to hide it. If all he wanted was a professional opinion, then why had he

said a few minutes ago that he had fallen in love with her?
Did that mean that he had fallen out of love as well?

She shrugged. 'If you insist.' She sat down cautiously
on the silver lace bedspread and opened the envelope.
'You're good. I can't see why you need my opinion,'
she muttered.

Mark stretched out beside her. 'You will,' he said
comfortably, and closed his eyes apparently ready to
wait as long as it took her to read the entire thing.

It took just a few pages before she knew what he had
done, and why there had been this silence between them
for a month. It was their story, and she read on, blindly
absorbed in how he had turned her search for Valerie
into a breathtaking book that would keep readers on
the edge of their chairs.

She laid aside the last page, and looked up,
bewildered. 'But it doesn't end, Mark,' she complained.
'It just stops!'

He raised up on one elbow. 'That's because I don't
know the ending, Shelby,' he said, very softly. 'Help
me?' He toyed with a lock of ash-blonde hair that
trailed over her shoulder.

'They have to be together,' she said breathlessly. 'It's
obvious that she loves him very much——'

'Is it?' he said quietly. 'I'm afraid it wasn't obvious at
all to me. She never said anything about loving him.'

'But I do,' she whispered. 'I mean—she does!'

His eyes were gleaming as he pulled her down beside
him, and his mouth was gentle as he caressed her.

'Oh, God, I think I fell in love with your letters,' she
confessed breathlessly. 'Before I ever came to Warren's
Grove at all.'

He grinned. 'I had an unfair advantage. But there
was still something about Shelby Stuart that made me
wonder. I wouldn't have come to New York, though. I
was too afraid that you'd have sixteen grand-
children——'

'Some day,' she said, very softly, 'we might.'

He buried his face in her hair. 'Shelby, can you bear to be married to a hack writer? We'll live wherever you want——'

'Even in New York?' She couldn't resist teasing him, just a little.

'Yes, if you want to keep your job. Now that Valerie's back to work again, Bob Jonas should be no challenge at all.'

Her heart was singing. He had listened and he had made it possible for her to keep the very job he hated, because she wanted to work. And suddenly it made the job a great deal less important to her.

'I don't intend to be without you ever again,' he said, and there was a promise in his voice.

Shelby sighed happily and relaxed in his arms. 'I'll never dare tell you that I have a headache,' she mused.

'Of course you can, dear heart,' he said, his voice muffled against her throat. 'I'll just cure it for you.' He stopped kissing her, reluctantly, and said, 'I suppose we'd better rejoin the world for a little while.'

'Give this up for a cocktail party?' She raised an eyebrow.

'No. For an announcement of an engagement.' He fumbled in his pocket. 'I thought you might like this.'

Shelby opened the tiny velvet box and gasped as a huge heart-shaped diamond, set in a gold band, winked up at her from the satin lining.

'It's perfect,' she said, and blinked away tears as he put it gently on to her finger.

Lora was sitting in a wing chair in the living-room, tapping her fingers on the arm. She was alone.

'Is the party over already?' Mark asked lightly.

Lora raised an elegant eyebrow. 'When I told you you could use my bedroom, Mark, I didn't realise that I should negotiate a ninety-nine year lease,' she jibed.

'Look, Lora.' Shelby held out her hand.

'Yes, I see that you have met the ladykiller, and he's yours.' She studied the diamond, and then looked suspiciously at Mark. 'I never expected it of you, Mark. And now—are you ready for the bad news?'

'Nothing could be bad news tonight,' Shelby told her.

'Perhaps not,' Lora admitted, 'especially since you now obviously have a new job, and you're no longer concerned about keeping Bob Jonas happy. It's Maria Martin, actually. She announced tonight that she's taking some time off to write a big novel. She'll be doing no more romances for Jonas Brothers.'

Mark's eyes met Shelby's. 'Here we go again,' he murmured. 'And after I went to all that work, too. *Oy vey, Maria*—! Just wait till I catch up with you!'

Shelby shook her head. 'No,' she said softly. 'I'll be plenty busy as Mrs Mark Buchanan—keeping my husband happy.'

He put one arm around her shoulders. 'In that case,' he murmured, 'shall we go do a little research on love scenes?'

'What about giving me back the twenty dollars I deposited in your savings account?' Shelby asked.

'What's mine is yours.' His tone was light, but Shelby knew he meant much more than that.

Lora rolled her eyes. 'My God,' she said. 'I expected it of Shelby—but for you to turn into a closet romantic on me, Mark——'

And then she looked puzzled as they collapsed into laughter in each other's arms.

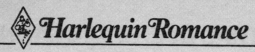

Harlequin Romance

Coming Next Month

Available in January wherever paperback books are sold, or
through Harlequin Reader Service.

In the U.S.
P.O. Box 1397
Buffalo, N.Y.
14240-1397

In Canada
P.O. Box 603
Fort Erie, Ontario
L2A 9Z9

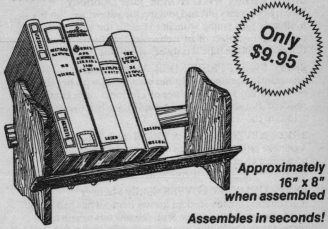

Here's how to get this special offer from Harlequin!

As simple as 1...2...3!

1. **Each month, save one Treasury Edition coupon from your favorite Romance or Presents novel.**

2. **In four months you'll have saved four Treasury Edition coupons (only one coupon per month allowed).**

3. **Then all you have to do is fill out and return the order form provided, along with the four Treasury Edition coupons required and $2.95 for postage and handling.**

Mail to: Harlequin Reader Service

In the U.S.A.	In Canada
901 Fuhrmann Blvd.	P.O. Box 609
P.O. Box 1397	Fort Erie, Ontario
Buffalo, NY 14240	L2A 9Z9

BN-Dec-2

Please send me my Special copy of the Betty Neels Treasury Edition. I have enclosed the four Treasury Edition coupons required and $2.95 for postage and handling along with this order form. (Please Print)

NAME_____

ADDRESS_____

CITY_____

STATE/PROV._____ ZIP/POSTAL CODE_____

SIGNATURE_____

This offer is limited to one order per household.

This special Betty Neels offer expires
February 28, 1987.

SUPPLIES LIMITED

Janet Dailey
Americana

Don't miss a single title from this great collection. The first eight titles have already been published. Complete and mail this coupon today to order books you may have missed.

Harlequin Reader Service

In U.S.A.
901 Fuhrmann Blvd.
P.O. Box 1397
Buffalo, N.Y. 14140

In Canada
P.O. Box 2800
Postal Station A
5170 Yonge Street
Willowdale, Ont. M2N 6J3

Please send me the following titles from the Janet Dailey Americana Collection. I am enclosing a check or money order for $2.75 for each book ordered, plus 75¢ for postage and handling.

_____	ALABAMA	Dangerous Masquerade
_____	ALASKA	Northern Magic
_____	ARIZONA	Sonora Sundown
_____	ARKANSAS	Valley of the Vapours
_____	CALIFORNIA	Fire and Ice
_____	COLORADO	After the Storm
_____	CONNECTICUT	Difficult Decision
_____	DELAWARE	The Matchmakers

Number of titles checked @ $2.75 each = $_____

N.Y. RESIDENTS ADD
APPROPRIATE SALES TAX $_____

Postage and Handling $____.75____

                                   TOTAL $_____

I enclose _____

(Please send check or money order. We cannot be responsible for cash sent through the mail.)

PLEASE PRINT

NAME _____

ADDRESS _____

CITY _____

STATE/PROV. _____

BLJD-A-1